COPERNICUS AVENUE

COPERNICUS AVENUE

ANDREW J. BORKOWSKI

stories

Cormorant Books

Canada Council   Conseil des Arts   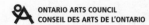 ONTARIO ARTS COUNCIL
for the Arts   du Canada   CONSEIL DES ARTS DE L'ONTARIO

Canadian Patrimoine   Canadä
Heritage canadien

The publisher gratefully acknowledges the support of the Canada Council for the Arts
and the Ontario Arts Council for its publishing program. We acknowledge the
financial support of the Government of Canada through the Canada Book Fund
(CBF) for our publishing activities, and the Government of Ontario through the
Ontario Media Development Corporation, an agency of the Ontario Ministry of
Culture, and the Ontario Book Publishing Tax Credit Program.

 The author received support from Ontario Arts Council, the Toronto
Arts Council, and the Canada Council for the Arts for the writing of
stories in this book.

Library and Archives Canada Cataloguing in Publication

Borkowski, Andrew J., 1956-
Copernicus Avenue / Andrew J. Borkowski.

Short stories.
ISBN 978-1-77086-001-8

1. Title.
PS8553.O734C66 2011   C813'.54   C2010-907353-3

Cover art and design: Angel Guerra/Archetype
Interior text design: Tannice Goddard, Soul Oasis Networking
Printer: Marquis

Printed and bound in Canada.

 RECYCLED   This book is printed on
Paper made from   100% post-consumer
recycled material   waste recycled paper.
FSC FSC® C021757
www.fsc.org

CORMORANT BOOKS INC.
215 SPADINA AVENUE, STUDIO 230, TORONTO, ONTARIO, CANADA M5T 2C7
www.cormorantbooks.com

To Peter and Alex, for being fabulous,
and to Martha, my partner, patron, and muse.

Contents

The Trees of Kleinsaltz

Oone early April morning, six years after their deportation, the inhabitants of the *Ulica 1 Maja* in Kleinsaltz, Lower Silesia, woke to find my great uncle, Stefan Mienkiewicz, hacking furiously at the apple tree in his garden. Stefan was a small man in a family of giants. But on this day he appeared fantastical and large in his anger, suspenders flailing at his waist like withered limbs.

"*Nie, nie, wujku,*" my uncles and cousins called. "Fruit or no, it's a fine tree, and so few of them left hereabouts. Look, it's almost in bloom."

But no one stopped him. This was his tree, his garden. And he was Stefan Mienkiewicz.

WHEN THE GERMANS CAME in the autumn of 1941, Stefan was reeve of Baranica, the marsh settlement founded by our family. The real leader of the community was my grandfather, Aleksander

Mienkiewicz, who was heir to the family estate and landlord of the entire district. The partisans had derailed a train a kilometre or two to the north, and an example had to be made. Aleksander was the obvious choice. So Stefan and the rest of our clan watched as my grandfather and seven of his ten sons were machine-gunned into a mass grave with their wives and children by an SS firing squad along with four hundred and fifty others. After the shooting stopped, the villagers stood still, under a spell, until my uncle turned from the pit's edge, looked the German commander in the eye, and said, "Can we go now? It looks like a good day coming. The barley won't harvest itself."

Stefan spent the next three years in a delicate balancing act. Every day, the German brigades demanded food and fuel. Every night, foraging parties from various partisan factions did the same. Both sides threatened to kill Stefan and everyone else in Baranica if they caught him supplying the others. His talent for shuffling livestock, like so many beads on an abacus, became a legend. There was a story of how he tricked a German quartermaster into requisitioning the same horse twice. There were tales of the mock partisans he trained to steal back food. "He has the power of loaves and fishes," the villagers said.

The miracles ended after the Red Army arrived. Disturbing reports filtered through from other settlements. Someone had gone to Karstwo and found the place empty, all things left where people had dropped them — a broom, a dish rag, a prayer book. The same scene was discovered at Ludowo and at Sarensk. The people of Baranica shuddered with a single thought: *Siberia*.

"That's the Russian way," some whispered. "Come in the night and drag you off without warning."

"It's true," countered others. "But it's better than the German way. They take you out and shoot you."

No one was surprised on the day a convoy of trucks arrived in Baranica and an NKVD man told what remained of the Mienkiewiczes and the other families that they had half an hour to gather whatever possessions they could carry. "You are going on a long journey," he said. "To a better place."

The young men spoke of resistance but Stefan scoffed at them.

"And what will you drive the Bolsheviks away with?" he asked. "Bulrushes?"

The Russians herded them into trucks and drove them to the stockyards at Minsk. They were loaded onto freight cars and shipped across their broken country to a station bearing the, name *Kleinsaltz*. After they disembarked, more Russians marched them along cobblestone streets that spilled through the town like dry creek beds. It was a small city built around what was left of a steel plant. But at its outskirts, peninsulas of houses thrust into meadows churned black by shells and tank treads. At the top of one of these, a sergeant said, "Here you are. Now go pick yourselves a new home."

The Russians were taking away the Mienkiewicz's marshes and giving them these strange German lowlands in exchange. The full meaning of it struck them only as they stood at the thresholds of the houses. Most had already been sacked by Russian soldiers; in a few, radios played a mix of military music and sombre, German-language bulletins. Cups of cold tea sat among stale kuchen left half-eaten on porcelain plates. Curtains, stirring at opened windows, gave an impression that they had been brushed by their fleeing German owners only seconds before.

Any deeper reflections were lost in the unbundling of lives. Houses flickered with strange lightning as children fingered electric switches. Other homes roared with the marvel of indoor plumbing. The shapes of lives were decided in half steps, by the speed with which a son could leap a fence and lay a claim. Brothers fought with brothers and mothers with daughters for the sake of a pantry or extra bed.

"Give up that mansion, old one. Everybody knows your daughters and their children are dead! They're in the pit back at Baranica."

"No, *cholera*. There's still my brother's family."

"From Pitowa? Ha! They're in the bottom of some Russian salt mine by now! Give it up, Grandpa!"

Stefan stilled these quarrels and, in the months that followed, he made sure the families put down roots in the strange new soil. He organized the men into gangs whose labour he sold in order to buy seeds and implements on the black market. He used the first few dollars from relatives in the West to bribe the Russian sappers into clearing the fields of mines. The crops that followed were abundant, with the earth enriched by so much burning (and, the men joked, by the rot of so many corpses). The fields were collectivized. Then the steel plant lurched back to life, taking many of the town away from the land for the first time in generations.

It struck them as curious that Stefan, who had always been more of an administrator than a farmer, chose this moment to become so passionate about his garden. He garnished it with a magnificence of sunflowers and hollyhocks, which, all summer long, were alive with bees from the hives of his nephew, Stanislaus Komarowski. In its first season it produced enough beans, tomatoes, carrots, onions, cucumbers, peas, and squash to feed himself and his wife through most of a winter.

The apple tree in his front garden was his main obsession. Each year it yielded a cloud of blossom and a thick canopy of leaf but no fruit. As time weighed more heavily on my great uncle's hands, his desire for a harvest of apples, for the taste of their tart, cool flesh, grew to a mania.

He went to the libraries of Wrocław and Poznań and returned

with the knowledge of blights and scales. He spent his days in the branches of the apple tree searching for signs of shot-hole, canker, or stinking smut. He inspected limbs twig by twig for some wound, perhaps the gouge of a German bullet, one that had served as a portal for disease. His shed became a dispensary for sulphates, hydrates, and arsenates that killed several chickens and a dog, but had no effect on the barren tree. As for my great uncle, the effort of climbing, the inhalation of the chemicals, and the long nights of study took their toll.

"What the Germans and the Russians could not do to Stefan Mienkiewicz," his neighbours said, "that tree will."

One day, as he sat pondering the distribution of scaffold branches around the apple tree's leader trunk, a voice addressed him in German.

"*Güten tag*. Is this the gentleman's house?"

"*Jawhol!*" answered Stefan, making out the wizened face that peered through the sunflower blossoms by the fence.

"I am curious," the stranger said. "You see, before the war, this was my house."

My great uncle was not a man of poetic gestures, but he knew that if any good were to be done the old German that day, it would have to be done by him.

"Of course, of course," he said. "Let me show you around."

He spent the afternoon reacquainting the visitor with his town, his fields, and his street. Shuffling the dirt with oversized, broken shoes, the old man recited the names of former occupants as he passed each house. When they came to the big stucco dwelling occupied by the Myczek family, he choked.

"This was the house of my parents. I was born in there."

The Myczeks had lost six cousins to the firing squad at Baranica. There was no sense in knocking.

My great uncle placed a hand on the German's shoulder. "You will dine with us and stay the night."

A turkey was slaughtered, and the old man was served as fine a meal as anyone on the street had eaten since before the war. Afterwards, Stefan opened a bottle of rectified *spiritus* vodka and the two men sat drinking and talking late into the night. The German told him of his family's expulsion from the town, the fate of those who resisted, the holding camps in East Germany.

"Such is the world we have known," countered my great uncle, "that the only comfort I can give you are stories of our own suffering." And he told the German his family's story. "But it's best to forget these things," he concluded. "Now we have new lives. It's a new world."

The old German shook his head. "It is easier for you." He waved a hand at a window that overlooked the garden. "You have been given paradise. It has been taken from us."

"It's true," ventured Stefan. "This is good land. But if the Russians would give us back our swamps and you these plains, we would accept." Then he tried to bridge the chasm between them with a joke. "And if this is a paradise, it's a strange one whose trees bear no fruit."

The old man's hollow eyes followed Stefan's to the apple tree shivering in moonlight.

"Three years I've worked on that tree. I've tried every remedy and still no apples."

The gnarled hands unclenched for a moment in the German's lap. "Yes, fruit trees can be difficult here. They are meant for higher ground than this."

Stefan nodded. "I've learned about that. But I wondered if it's something in the earth, some pest buried so deep it can't be detected."

"My people worked this land for two hundred years," said the German. "We know its tricks."

"And the tree? You have the answer to that?"

"Yes. I have the answer. Why shouldn't I share it with you? It won't do us much good in Leipzig. Tomorrow, before I go, I'll write out my little remedy."

The next morning, Stefan woke early, excited at the prospect of a cure for the tree. But the German was gone. His bed had not been slept in. There was a note on the kitchen table. Stefan took it up and read:

> When my sons return to Kleinsaltz and hang your sons from the branches of the apple tree in my garden, then it will bear fruit.
> — R. Richter

The note had scarcely settled back on the table before Stefan Mienkiewicz was searching for his axe. Moments after finding it, he attacked the tree's trunk, his thinning hair turned upwards in gossamer horns. His clansmen watched dumbstruck until the tree fell and Stefan trudged back to his bed, chilled and delirious. After one of his sons found the note and had it read to the crowd by a cousin who knew German, the men went to their sheds and cellars and returned with axes in hand. They set upon the stump and roots, hacking and sawing until all trace of the tree was gone from Stefan's garden. That night they burned the branches, brush, stump, and roots on the meadow behind the house. Never, the men said afterwards, had a fire thrown such heat.

Allemande Left

From the northwest corner, Thadeus can see the length of the Avenue. Two- and three-storey buildings line either side, facades capped with tentative peaks and modest spires that conceal a baldness of flat roofs. The scene is lashed down with streetcar wires that force the eye to the blue abyss of the lake at the Avenue's root.

When Thadeus looks closer (which, he has learned, Torontonians rarely do) he sees that the street is a subtle riot of styles. Here at the corner of Howard Park, a drugstore opposite him squats under a mansard roof dormered with oval-windowed gables in the Empire style. The treetops that bunch over the surrounding streets are broken by the wrinkled hides of protestant bell towers that tilt toward the Gothic, the Romanesque, the Norman, and the baroque, sometimes mixing all four. About halfway down to the water, St. Bridget's Catholic Church crouches behind its Corinthian columns and stone portico. They have a thing for Greek temples, these Torontonians.

The Dominion bank on the corner opposite is a miniature Parthenon. The Revue cinema a few doors down has faux pillars and reliefs pressed into the stucco above its marquee. Castles, too. On the north corner is the Joy Oil gas station, shaped like a tiny chateau with conical turret, leaded windows, and steep clay-tiled roof. A few doors up, the clock tower of G.W. Patterson's funeral home counts off the hours above crenellated parapets.

This is his neighbourhood now, the last wide avenue of the downtown, the border between city and suburb. When Thadeus tries to explain where he lives, even to people who've lived in the city their whole lives, no one can picture where he means. The Avenue is a neighbourhood between neighbourhoods. Parkdale to the east, High Park to the west: everyone knows these, but not the Avenue. King and Queen streets end at its bottom. To the northeast, the rail corridor cuts the city's regulated grid, causing Dundas and College to merge and veer north on a diagonal, while side streets convulse in a tangle of dead ends. It's a nameless buffer zone, the perfect receptacle for Thadeus and his army of displaced persons from another place-between-places. Poland, the ultimate buffer state.

"The last city in the last country on earth I will ever choose to live in." Thadeus remembers thinking this as the Royal York and the Imperial Bank slid from his view aboard the train taking him to Halifax and the troopship back to England in '43. It wasn't just the interminable Sundays — bereft of movies, sports, and alcohol, ordained to humiliate those without homes or families — that had made him feel this way. It wasn't just the sweaty beer parlours engineered to elicit shame in the hearts of their patrons, the Orange Day parades, or the "Gentiles Only" signs at the beaches. It was what he sees now, as he looks down the Avenue of faux cathedrals, temples, and chateaux: a city's stubborn ignorance of itself, it's refusal to be.

THE SISTERS LINE UP at the sink to do the dishes and Harriet, the youngest, she of the golden voice, has them singing along with the radio. There's an Andrews Sisters retrospective playing, and even sourpuss Mary-Katherine, the eldest, is chipping in a harmony and twirling her dishtowel to "Don't Sit Under the Apple Tree." Back when that song was new, Marlene would have been in the thick of it, lifting her voice alongside her sisters, happy to be home on leave, bobbing to the music in her WAAF uniform.

"C'mon, Mar. M-K needs help on the alto part."

That was a long time ago. Five years since the end of the war, seven since she and Fletch saw the Andrews Sisters at the Palace Pier. Now all she wants is order, to gather up the debris the nieces and nephews have strewn around the parlour. She collects the playing cards that have been serving as letters posted through the slotted seat of Dad's oak footstool. She rights the stool and restores it to its place in front of his rocker. She folds the weekend paper into the magazine rack, where Dad would have expected it to be, and arranges the articles on his side table, pipe, ashtray carved from the hollowed bole of an elm, and the Marine Band harmonica in its bright, filigreed box.

She tries to picture her dad the way Father McAulay described him at the funeral, raising his harmonica among the heavenly hosts, eyes twinkling with Irish mischief. He wouldn't have wanted her to be here on her own, clinging to her memories, any more than he had wanted her living with him after she was demobbed, playing the spinster, looking after her ailing father. Dad had tended her with books and music and tall tales during the year when her nerves forced her to stay home from school, and he had always encouraged her to get out of her shell.

"Go!" he had said when she announced her plan to make a new beginning by joining the WAAF back in '41. "Go see the world."

They stationed her on a base in tobacco country north of Lake Erie and assigned her to kitchen patrol. Not much world to see there, but the world came to her. Australians, New Zealanders, South Africans, Texans, even a few Sikhs from India, all came to learn to fly in the flak-free skies of Ontario. Above all, there was Fletch, a real cowboy from Alberta with a Harvard trainer for a stallion, sweeping her round the sky as deftly as he did around the dance floor at Port Stanley on the night he proposed. After the war, he said, he'd take her home to the foothills, and he talked of little else in his letters home after he shipped out to Europe.

It only took one visit to the locked ward at Sunnybrook Hospital, where they kept Fletch after he came back, to know that she'd never see those foothills. A nurse told her that it had been shrapnel, a single fragment piercing his canopy over Holland, two weeks before the war's end. The British surgeons had done their best, a miracle that anyone could survive a head wound like that. They moved him west to a facility near Lethbridge, where he'd be closer to his family. Neither of the families had known about the engagement. He being a Protestant and she a Catholic, they had planned to elope.

She kept the ring in its box on her dresser and turned to her Dad, devoted herself to him the same way he had devoted himself to her until his heart, enlarged with years of working in the heat of the foundries, had given out.

Marlene is straightening the volumes of Dickens and George Eliot in Dad's bookcase when M-K breezes in from the kitchen.

"The men want coffee, Mar. Where are those mugs I gave you?"

"Oh, I put them away. In the fruit cellar. Dad never liked those mugs with the dark glazes. He said you could never see the coffee in them."

M-K draws in a sharp breath.

"Dad's been gone almost a year, Mar."

"I know."

"I gave you those mugs three weeks ago."

THE CAFÉ BAMBI IS two doors down from the Revue, its ersatz timbers strung with the flags of Switzerland, France, Austria, and the new German Federal Republic. The café is one of several businesses — Schultz's Meats, Mannheim Music, and Dresdner Arts & Crafts — that make up the Avenue's tiny German enclave in the blocks south of Howard Park.

"Funny," says Pavel Skrubicki as he spikes his coffee in one of the Bambi's padded booths. "Five years the war is over and everywhere we go, we're still chasing out the Germans."

True. In Manitoba, they took the place of German prisoners of war on the beet farms. Armed guards ("Zombies," the Canadians called them, draftees who refused to volunteer for service overseas) had marched the Poles from the train station in St. Boniface out to the unheated sheds that, a few weeks earlier, had housed the POWs. It felt like they were being swept under the carpet, kept out of sight in a Canadian Siberia. Toronto felt good after that and, yes, it felt like small justice to be crowding the German clientele out of places like the Café Bambi.

Thadeus scans the Sunday afternoon gathering of DPs sporting the boxy demob suits that Canadian vets consigned to the Crippled Civilians shop long ago, steeped in the fumes of acrid Balkan tobacco. It's the intellectuals who fare the worst. The Canadians want coal miners and farm boys to do the heavy lifting their own men are no longer willing to do. The architects, the lawyers, the doctors, and the teachers have had to conceal their educations from the immigration officers, just as they did from the Gestapo and the Soviet secret police, the NKVD, exaggerating time spent on the farms of distant relatives or playing up their experience cutting trees in the Gulag. And now they are the ones who must make a single cup of coffee last an afternoon, while labourers like Mieczysław Lobinski get work digging out the trench for the city's new subway line and who top up their income by arm wrestling at the Bambi's back table.

Men like Pavel Skrubicki are also thriving. Skrubicki is said to have done well in the postwar black market, brags of arriving in Canada with fifty thousand US dollars sewn into the lining of his trench coat, has already bought himself a house in Parkdale where he rents rooms to his less fortunate compatriots, and spends four afternoons a week at the racetrack.

"Pan Tadeusz to the rescue!" he cries when he sees Thadeus in the doorway. "Come, sit here. Save me from this."

He gestures at the spectre of Ignacy Poniatowski, fixed to the banquette opposite him, gloved fingers folded around the demitasse he has been nursing. Thadeus has never seen Poniatowski out of his blue topcoat with sable collar, or without a white silk scarf folded at his throat and the dove-grey homburg hat to match his gloves. He claims he must dress warmly to offset damage done to his circulatory system during the war, though it's not clear whether said damage was incurred at the hands of the Gestapo or in a Kazakh labour camp. Everyone is free to invent their own story here, and no one is entirely sure of Poniatowski, who claims to be an official delegate of the government in exile.

He and Skrubicki are in another of their standoffs. The latter gnaws at a platter of schnitzel. The former looks on, lips pursed beneath waxed moustaches.

"Pan Poniatowski has been a very busy man, Tadek," says Skrubicki through a mouthful of dumplings.

"Pan Poniatowski *is* a very busy man. And what's occupying him now?"

"I must go to Ottawa," says Poniatowski.

"Why?"

"So he can spend a week in the Chateau Laurier," Skrubicki interjects, "while the minister of external affairs spends a week refusing to see him."

"We must maintain pressure on the government to denounce the elections of '48 and break off relations with the communists."

"You are crazy. This is Canada, my friend. In Ottawa, they don't even fart unless the British or the Americans do it first. You're best staying away from Ottawa. You know it's the venereal disease capital of Canada."

Skrubicki hails the waitress as she brushes past their table. "*Bitte meine frau!* Apple juice for these gentlemen."

"I think I'd prefer a coffee."

"No, Tadek. It's apple juice you want."

After the glasses arrive and the waitress is out of sight, Skrubicki takes up the paper bag at his side and peels back the paper to show a bottle of greenish liquid, the familiar bison glowering from the label.

"Żubrówka!"

"The real bison grass vodka, my friend. They're making it again, in Białystok."

"Where did you get it?"

"Your friend has been fraternizing," Poniatowski intones. "That's where he got it."

"Fraternizing? With who?"

"Those bandits at the consulate."

"Heh-heh. They may be communists, those bastards, but they know a good business proposition when they see it."

"So they give you vodka, and what do you give them?"

"What do you think? *Dolary!* Two dollars a bottle. I can sell it here on Copernicus Avenue for five."

"And what will it be next, Pavel? Information for your vodka?"

"The war is over, Grandad. We lost. Remember?"

"Correction," Poniatowski gestures at a Canadian couple studying a display of baby clothes in a shop window across the Avenue. "Their war is over. Ours is not."

"Well, mine ended the day they screwed us over at Yalta. Since then, nothing makes sense except this ...," he waves a sheaf of dollar bills "... and this." He lifts the bottle to pour. "You want some?"

Poniatowski lifts a gloved hand in refusal.

"*Na zdrowie*, Tadek." Skrubicki clinks glasses with Thadeus, downs his drink at gulp and rises. "Pan Poniatowski. You may not think me fit to lift a drink with, but you like my money well enough when it comes to funding these crusades of yours. Everything has changed. Your world is finished. No more swaggering around Piccadilly with gold braid on your collar. You're just like the rest of us, just another DP with nothing but the clothes on his back. You had your chance, you and your colonels. You can play Don Quixote all you want. Go to Ottawa, tilt at all the windmills you can find. Just don't expect any of us to be your Sancho Panza. We're done with that. Now, if you'll excuse me gents, I think I'll join the living."

Skrubicki insinuates himself into a table of card players who are more likely to part with their meagre pension money for a taste of home than for any scheme of Poniatowski's.

"We must be careful of men like that, Tadek."

"Well, he's right about Ottawa. They warned us about the hookers when I was there during the war."

"Men like Skrubicki are easily turned. Did you know he was in the *Wehrmacht?*"

"Of course, they incorporated his hometown into the Reich so they drafted him. He surrendered first chance he got and joined our side."

"If he keeps dealing with those vermin at the consulate, they'll turn him. You've seen how the NKVD works, Pan Mienkiewicz."

"Spies in our midst. You sound like Mr. Gouzenko. Be careful or they'll be putting a bag over *your* head next."

"We owe a great deal to Gouzenko. Since he defected, it hasn't been so easy for those Canadian communists and their Tim Buck to call us fascists and warmongers. Thanks to Gouzenko and this war in Korea, people are waking up. And men like you and I, Pan Mienkiewicz, we have work to do."

Thadeus realizes he's been duped. Skrubicki has used the offer of a drink as a ploy to extract himself from Poniatowski's company. He scans the room for other potential Sancho Panzas to take his place, but none offer themselves. He's stuck with a man who has but one topic of conversation, a topic that everyone is weary of.

"And what projects are you hatching now?"

"Education. We must tell our story. I am writing letters, papers, articles in the *Głos Polski*. Pan Tadeusz, you were a schoolteacher, an educator. We could use a man with your qualifications."

"Pan Poniatowski, I taught the children of goatherds to spell their names in Ukrainian. I am not a lobbyist. That's a job for you politicians."

"Entertainment, then. I am going into the movie business."

"You?"

"I am planning a series of films to be shown at the Brighton theatre down the street. They are making fine pictures now: *The Red Menace*, *Guilty of Treason*. We need leaflets, advertising."

Poniatowski's skin is like yellowed paper, suggesting a jaundice contracted somewhere in his travels. He looks frail under his ill-fitting coat.

"This also is a chance for you to educate, to undo all the damage those communists in Hollywood did before they were found out ..."

Thadeus wonders if he has enough change to buy the man something to eat and how he can make the man accept his charity.

"It is because of them that the world thought Stalin was the great benefactor even as he put the heroes of the Uprising on trial as bandits."

He could order the soup for himself then claim not to be hungry but Poniatowski would simply insist he send it back.

"Senator McCarthy hasn't even scratched the surface! We must continue the fight, Pan Mienkiewicz. We cannot rest until Warsaw is ours again."

Thadeus draws back as Poniatowski jumps to his feet and lances the air with his stick.

"I demand to know who is with me and who are the traitors in this room!"

The restaurant goes silent. Wisps of cigarette smoke are the only things that move. The card players freeze in mid-hand and Mieczysław Lobinski, momentarily distracted, allows his opponent to force his arm to the table.

The butt of Poniatowski's cane comes to rest on a vector that ends between Skrubicki's broad shoulders. The gambler rounds on his accuser, drawing his fingers into beefy knots. Thadeus gently extends a hand and closes it around the man's wrist, just above the cuff of his dove-grey glove, feels the brittleness of bones that could snap with the flick of a finger.

"Sit down, old chap. I think you've made your point."

Poniatowski melts into his seat. The defiance in his eyes flushed away by shame for his failure to prevent what has befallen every man in this room. Thadeus signals for everyone to go back to their games, then gives his friend a moment to compose himself.

"You are right, Pan Poniatowski, we continue the fight," says Thadeus. "But not in this way. I have seen the newsreels of the show trials in Moscow and I know how the Russians work. I think of them every time I read about how your Senator McCarthy works, or about that secret commission in Ottawa after Gouzenko. We did not fight to put men on trial for what they believe in, Ignacy. It's everything we fought against."

"And what do you propose, Pan Mienkiewicz?"

"We make the most of the victory that's been given to us."

"And what victory is that?"

"Life, my friend. We defy them — everyone who has tried so hard to kill us — because we *live*. So why don't we start with some lunch?"

THE WESTERN GATES OF the new stadium swing open. Snare drums rattle and the colour guard of the De La Salle Band, feathered with Union Jacks and Red Ensigns and the crossed keys of the papal banner, struts onto the field. Horns strike into a martial rendition of "O Mary We Crown Thee," setting a cadence for the girls of St. Joseph's College School who march behind wearing mortar boards and the black uniforms of novices. The nurses of St. Mike's and St. Joe's hospitals come dazzling behind them in red satin capes, followed by the sashed and sabre-decked Knights of Columbus and beribboned officers of the Holy Name Society (Confraternity of the Holy Names of God and Jesus, loyal to the Magisterium of the Holy Catholic Church, consecrated to perpetual acts of reverence and works of Mercy corporal and spiritual). All march with rosaries bunched in their swinging fists. Finally come the massed ranks of the clergy, Diocesans, Basilians, Oblates, Jesuits, Franciscans, Sisters of Loreto and St. Joseph, De La Salle Brothers, and Brothers of the Blessed Order of St. John.

It's Rosary Hour in the city of Toronto, the first time the event has been held at the new CNE Grandstand. Forty rows up, Marlene sits with her sister Mary-Katherine. She can see everything from here: City Hall's gothic spire, the Imperial Bank of Commerce tower (tallest in the Empire), the Royal York in its mitre of green copper, all facing the waterfront as if trying to ignore the spectacle of twenty thousand Catholics massed in the open air. It's a far cry from Rosary Hours before the war, when the community barricaded itself in the old baseball stadium behind Tip Top Tailors, its beams and timbers a shield against the watchful eye of the Orange Lodge. Back then, men like Marlene's father couldn't get work building Maple Leaf Gardens because they were Catholics. Now, King Clancy and the Leafs' coach, Joe Primeau, are right there on the podium for the whole city to see.

Bishop Dignan, in gold-embroidered chasuble and matching mitre, gives the assembly his benediction, reads the story of Lazarus from the Gospel according to St. John, and begins his homily.

"The Catholic population of Toronto has literally arisen and walked in a glorious manifestation of love and devotion to God and His Immaculate Mother. We are not unaware that there are those who look askance at our love for the Mothers of Christ. Let them reflect on the appalling fact of history that those who have begun by rejecting the Blessed Mother, have ended by rejecting her Divine Son."

The girls of St. Joseph's fan out across the midfield and gather themselves into knots of five to form the beads of the Living Rosary, linked by strands of white linen in a chain which shapes the Immaculate Heart of Mary. At the centre, the girls configure a white crucifix with broad sheets. One of them, shoulders draped in red satin, takes her station at the head of the cross as the rector of St. Michael's Cathedral moves to the microphone and begins his recitation of the Apostles' Creed.

"I believe in God, the Father almighty, creator of heaven and earth. I believe in Jesus Christ, His only son, Our Lord ..."

M-K is instantly intent, pinched into the forgetfulness of faith, in a place where Marlene can't follow. Before the war, the family thought that she, their youngest, would be the one with a vocation, become a bride of the Church. She had gone to confession every week, said the rosary every night on the living room floor with her mother. Her favourite devotion had been the blessing of throats on the feast of Saint Blaise.

"He descended into hell. On the third day He rose again. He ascended into heaven and is seated at the right hand of the Father ..."

A plane flies over, one of the new airliners bound for Malton. Its cruciform shadow cuts the Living Rosary on a diagonal. Marlene listens for a false note in the moan of its engines, looks up to assess its grip on the air, a reflex she picked up in the air force. Even though they were four thousand miles from the fighting, there were so many things that could go wrong and did. Faith came in handy. On their last night together, she had given Fletch a St. Christopher's medal for his instrument panel.

"I believe in the Holy Catholic Church, the communion of saints, the forgiveness of sins, the resurrection of the body, and life everlasting. Amen."

The red-caped girl who serves as a marker moves up from the crucifix and along the first four beads of the Living Rosary. Twenty thousand voices murmur the Our Father and three Hail Marys. Italians, Hungarians, Poles, and Lithuanians spice the prayers with fresh accents and strange grace notes. This is the Church triumphant, not just the refuge of the Catholic Irish and Scots, its ranks swollen by wave after wave of DPs. The marker moves on from the bead representing the cycle's lone Glory Be to the Father as the rector announces the rosary's opening decade.

"The First Glorious Mystery. The Resurrection."

Marlene fumbles for the beads that have lain in the bottom of her purse since Dad's funeral, takes them up, observes the forms. This is M-K's idea of getting her "back out into the world." But she knows what M-K wants. She's brought Marlene here in the hope of rekindling her vocation, a handy way to get her out of their father's house. "The Sisters will still have you, Mar. Even at your age. You just have to be willing to repent." M-K has heard the stories of what went on during the war, in rooms of the Edgewater Hotel, in the backs of jeeps and transports, on the kitchen tables of Parkdale butchers. This is what she suspects Marlene of, with Fletch.

"The Second Glorious Mystery. The Ascension."

But Marlene has nothing to repent. There was only Fletch, and he had been decent with her. After word of his crash had come from a squadron-mate in England, and for months after her agonizing last visit to Sunnybrook, her faith was nothing but a hot iron in her side, with Father Boyle rasping on the other side of the confessional screen that it was all God's judgment.

"The Third Glorious Mystery. The Descent of the Holy Spirit."

She refused to do her penance, hasn't been to confession since. Her time with Fletch was no sin, and she has nothing further to confess. So she stands at M-K's side, observes the forms, shapes the words without sounding them.

FRAN'S HASN'T CHANGED SINCE the war. Plump waitresses in uniforms that hug all the wrong curves still sling plates of overcooked food they call "hash" between cramped booths that discourage loitering. But you can linger at the counter as long as you have a coffee cup and a newspaper in front of you.

The *Star* has a picture of the previous day's rosary at Exhibition

Stadium on its front page, young girls linked in the shape of a heart on a football field. The rest of the news is from Korea, where General MacArthur's forces have penetrated thirty miles into the North and US B-29s are under orders to stay clear of the Chinese border on their bomb runs.

On page four there's an item about marine mutations in the Bikini atoll, four years after the nuclear test. "Fantastic Forms of Fish Said Result of Atomic Bombing." The bomb has changed everything, even the fish. Buried at the bottom of page ten is a piece that will stoke Poniatowski's righteous anger: "Pickets in Protest of Polish General." General Anders is in New York and the American Labour Party "and other groups" are protesting outside his hotel. According to the protesters, the hero of Monte Cassino is "a war criminal and a partner of Hitler." At a press conference, the baffled general says the charges are "incomprehensible."

Thadeus has another battle to fight, his next objective being a stone office tower on University Avenue. He walks west, past the temples and cathedrals of the university in the shade of huge maples. He passes the hospital where a Canadian surgeon fixed his broken nose by flattening it. Sir John A. Macdonald's statue, with Queen Victoria looking on through the trees, scowls over Thadeus's shoulder as he turns down University Avenue at Queen's Park and makes for the Dominion Life Assurance Company of Canada, where he is interviewed by a Mr. Samuels in an office that smells of old paper and pipe smoke.

"Your service record of service is impressive, Mr. Mankawhiz."

Don't correct his pronunciation. Don't ask about his service record, either. There are no photos of aircraft or warships or tanks in Mr. Samuels' office, no regimental or Legion insignia on his lapel. Thadeus knows the reasons these men offer up: heart murmur, flat feet, age — none of which would have been an excuse in the Polish forces.

"You started the war as a — I'm sorry, does this say Lancer?"

"Yes."

"And what exactly was a Lancer."

"It was the cavalry." Thadeus should take this off his resume. Mr. Samuels is now trying to picture him with sabre raised, charging wild-eyed at a phalanx of German panzers.

"But you finished the war under British command."

"Yes, in the Air Force. Polish Air Force, but British command." It's important to stress the British thing. Last week he went to city hall to apply for a clerk's position; they may as well have put "citizens of British ancestry only" right on the application. "I was coming to Toronto for training in 1942 and 1943. I was navigator, much mathematics, meteorology, and working radar machines."

"And before the war you were a teacher. Why aren't you trying to pursue that line of work here in Canada?"

"Aha. No. You see. My English."

The interview continues for another ten minutes, but Thadeus can tell, from Mr. Samuels' slow, emphatic phrases, that he's given the Dominion Life Assurance Company all the reasons it needs to dismiss his application. The veterans who matter all have jobs by now. He'll need something more than a war on his resume to win this battle.

THE STREETCAR LAUNCHES ITSELF across the viaduct bridging the Don Valley. This side of the city is strange territory to Thadeus. The valley pulses with autumnal oranges and reds in the sunset, like the burning cities he's viewed from thirty thousand feet. Lights are already on in the farmhouses and small industrial works that dot the valley floor. He hasn't explored these valleys and ravines that squiggle down out of the wilderness to infiltrate the city. Thadeus has noticed that all Canadian cities have some natural feature that dwarfs or sub-verts them, reminds them who's boss. Montreal has its mountain, Winnipeg has its river which, just this spring, flooded thousands of people out of their homes, and Toronto has these wild channels that pull the rug from under its meticulously planned streetscape. The north wind buffets the streetcar, and for a second Thadeus feels like he's airborne again, taking in the countryside from the Perspex dome of an Avro Anson out of Malton, astrolabe in hand, getting his bearings over Tamworth, Peterborough, Arnprior, banking north over lakes scattered like tarnished coins in the moonlight. So much water. So much nothing.

The streetcar takes cover between shoebox-shaped storefronts on Danforth Avenue. Thadeus gets off at Broadview and walks north into a neighbourhood where chinless houses give way to chicken coops, a stable yard, and slouching, vaguely sinister machine shops. The smell of dung vies with diesel fumes for control of the chill autumn air as he reaches Pottery Road and turns down a street that is little more than a cart track. The road folds a couple of wooden farmhouses into its bends. A small foundry with square chimney clanks and hisses on the valley floor. He senses the presence of horses, but the only one visible is the cement stallion that rears over a sign that names his destination: "Fantasy Farm."

"YOU'LL HAVE THE DICKENS of a time dancing in that getup, Mar."

It's true. In her pencil skirt, heels, and bolero jacket, Marlene is completely out of step and the dancing hasn't even begun. The other women (Marlene has to remind herself that they're no longer girls — most of them are married), in gingham bows and petticoats three or four layers deep under their dresses, look like prize cauliflowers trussed up for a harvest festival. The men wear stetsons and string ties and distinguish themselves as either "dudes" or "regular guys" by the way they tuck their cuffs into their cowboy boots. A couple of them straighten the Air Force Association crest on the wall behind the bandstand where musicians tune guitars and fiddles. Others finish moving tables into place around the dance floor periphery, then adjourn to the bar to pluck bottles of Dow's ale from an ice-filled tub.

Ruth McKay is right. She won't be able to budge in this outfit. Ruth had even warned her to wear flat shoes and something loose. What was she thinking? She hadn't wanted to come, she let Ruth put her up to it. Why? To satisfy M-K that she's doing something to get herself out? At least in square dancing, she thought, you don't have sit like a wallflower waiting for someone to ask you to dance. But here she is again, sabotaging herself, dressing to guarantee her exile to the kitchen with the other spinsters, because that's what she is.

She tries to make herself useful, fashioning centrepieces from ears of Indian corn, hanks of straw, and the rust-coloured leaves she has gathered from the lawn out back.

"Pssst."

Ruth startles her with a nudge and a nod toward the coat check, where a tall thin man is handing off his overcoat and silk scarf. In his greenish grey sharkskin suit and striped bowtie, he looks more of a misfit than Marlene, a throwback to the thirties. Clipped moustache, high forehead, and slicked-back hair, like John Barrymore in *Grand Hotel*, except for the flattened nose. She'd guess he was a boxer if the rest of him weren't so slender.

"Hang on to your hemline, Mar," says Ruth. "The Polacks are here."

WHEN HE SEES THE men dressed like lumberjacks with shoelaces for ties, and the women puffed up and frilled like turkey hens, he realizes that he is out of his element. His English has betrayed him again: he thought the square dance advertised in the Air Force Association Bulletin would feature a big band in a public square. A little liquid courage is in order. Not much chance of a cognac, but maybe some good Canadian whisky. Alas, all that's on offer is their beer that tastes like battery acid and makes him fart. The men stand drinking it — as Canadian men are wont to do — straight out of the bottle. He finds the practice repulsive, but he reminds himself that he is a Canadian now, so he does as the Canadians do. He drinks, lets the amber foam scour his throat, and he listens intently, trying to pick up the thread of the men's conversation. Of course, they are talking about hockey. The Toronto Maple Leafs are about to start their new season and the men seem very concerned that they have revenge for a terrible defeat the year before at the hands of the Red Wings of Detroit. Names pass among them like the names of saints: Bentley, Kennedy, Smith, Meeker, Barilko. They mean nothing to Thadeus. During the war, some businessmen from the King Eddie took him to a game at Maple Leaf Gardens against the Canadiens from Montreal. It was the most brutal thing he'd witnessed outside the field of battle. Three players had to be carried from the ice with faces cut and broken, blood pouring down their jerseys, before the game ended in a brawl. It took the referees half an hour to pull the players, grown men tussling like boys, off one another as the crowd shouted down abuse on the visitors, whom his hosts referred to as "the Frenchies." All the while, ushers patrolled the aisles, ready to expel any man who wasn't wearing a tie. Thadeus marvelled at the fact that a people as subdued and easygoing as Canadians could make a passion of this most violent of games.

He betrays none of his bewilderment to the men at the bar. He nods, sips his beer, and waits for an opening in the conversation, which comes when the subject turns to the future of the Leafs' veteran goaltender, Turk Broda.

"Ah, Broda! He is my countryman, is he not?"

The veterans trade startled glances until one of them says, "Yeah that's right. Broda's a polack." And so, thanks to the burly guardian of the Leafs' net, Thadeus is granted admission to this small circle of Canadian manhood. He withdraws his silver cigarette case and offers it around, asks them about their wartime service, but most of them were either ground crew or fliers who never made it out of Canada. The war is already a distant memory. The conversation veers back to cars and houses and wives and kids. So he's relieved when a man in an embroidered jacket invites newcomers to the floor for instructions on the fundamentals of square dancing. Do-si-do, allemande left, roll the barrel, tap the keg, chase the rabbit: only a few flecks of the instructor's English stick to his memory after the lesson is finished. Thadeus will trust his instincts. How different can it be from a Krakowiak or a Mazurka? He removes his jacket and rolls up his sleeves, the better to fit in with these lumberjacks.

The dancers fall in to squares of four couples. Most have regular partners: husbands, wives, fiancés. A chubby woman who must have held rank in the air force judging by the way she ropes strays into formation, directs Thadeus and another single man to an unfinished square at the back of the floor.

"It seems all the ladies are taken," she says as if this is somehow the fault of the men. "I'll see if there are some hiding in the kitchen."

She returns with a girl in tow. Reddish-brown hair, curled and swept back into wings that frame a pair of startled green eyes set over lightly freckled cheekbones flushed with embarrassment. The girl flutters in the big woman's slipstream, stocking feet mincing over the polished floorboards. Her clothes, a slender skirt and mauve blouse, are every bit as inappropriate as his. Slight, frail, a damsel in distress, Thadeus's specialty. He readies the words that will put the poor girl at her ease.

The commandante doesn't deliver her captive to Thadeus; she presents her to the other fellow, who stands gaunt and fearful on his right.

"You," says the commandante as she places Thadeus's arm in a military policeman's grip, "shall be *my* partner."

The fiddle player steps to the front of the stage and swings the band into a skirl of the screeching Don Messer music that grates in his ears.

"Bow to your partner. Bow to your corner," calls the man in the embroidered jacket and the whole floor is in motion. Dancers pivot and weave like the folds of a paper puzzle, air foaming with gingham and lace, the floor pulsing with the beat of high-heeled boots. The caller tells him to wipe off his tie and pull down his vest, to chase rabbits and squirrels, open a book and write a cheque. Thadeus has no idea what any of it means. He just follows his instincts as the commandante manoeuvres around him with drill-hall precision. He swings his partner, he do-si-dos, does it all with more energy and lift than most of the men on the floor. He has left behind Poniatowski and the Copernicus Avenue set, all the ones who insist on walking backwards into their new home. He will learn to skate, have sons who play baseball. He will own a house in the new suburbs, a car, and a driveway to park it in. He will lose his accent and finish his sentences with "eh?"

Caught up in the forward rush of his imagination, he forgets the barefoot young woman who bobs tentatively around her helpless partner on his right.

"Allemande left!"

"MARLENE, I AM SO sorry. You'd think he'd at least know his right from his left."

Worse than the bump that is now rising over her left eyebrow, worse than the run in her stocking, worse even than the tear to the seam of her new skirt, is all these people fussing over her. But the ringleaders of the association auxiliary, Fran Beardsley, Rene MacCulloch, and Tilly Haines, who've never paid her the least bit of attention, have to outdo one another with shows of concern.

"Are you really all right dear?"

"Are you sure you didn't black out?"

"Quite sure thanks. We bumped heads is all. Then I lost my balance."

"I'm sorry I let that oaf near you."

"He's not an oaf. He's a good dancer. You were his partner, Tilly. You should know."

She glances over Tilly Haines's shoulder to where the Polish man stands at a respectful distance, lips pursed in a slightly pained expression, hands working a little pathetically at his side. He sports a welt corresponding to hers over his left eye. When Ruth McKay brings her a fresh compress, she nods in the direction of the Pole and says, "I'm fine. Maybe you should offer it to him."

He waves away the proffered cloth, but takes it as an opening, and edges through Marlene's unwanted circle of protection. The women step away to what seems a safe distance, as if he were about to explode. Instead, the Pole draws himself up, clicks his heels and bows sharply from the waist. Then he takes up her hand and brushes the knuckles of her index and middle fingers with his lips.

"Young lady," he croons. "I am asking forgiveness. In England I am a navigator. But in Canada, my navigation is not so good. Maybe I am thinking 'port' and 'starboard,' not 'left' and 'right.'"

"You are forgiven, sir," Marlene answers. "I see you have a bump too. Are you all right?"

He taps his flattened nose with an index finger.

"I have suffered much worse. As you can see."

"I hadn't noticed," she lies.

He bows again and withdraws toward the bar.

"I'll say one thing," Tilly Haines observes dryly as she watches him disappear. "They sure know how to turn it on."

THE DANCERS MOVE OUTSIDE where there is a wishing well and a fire already blazing five feet high. He stands by the fire, where he thinks most people will gather, but they stay by the long trestle table where cobs of corn are being served on paper plates. The misadventure on the dance floor has set him further apart than ever from the rest of the partygoers. His demob overcoat and snap brim Trilby stand out among the toques and plaid woollens. Perhaps this was a mistake. Perhaps he should go. He checks his watch, the air-force-issue Omega with radium-painted hands and numbers that glow greenly in the shadows. It's only nine o'clock. Still time to cross town to the Palais Royale, where the Combatants are throwing a dance to introduce vets to the latest group of Polish girls to arrive from the refugee camps in Austria. But no. He stands his ground, smokes with all the elegance he can muster, and waits for a chance to redeem himself.

"Would you like some?"

The woman he collided with stands in front of him, offering a plate. Thadeus stares at the steaming cob. It's something he can't seem to acquire, this Canadian taste for cattle feed. But he sees his opportunity and takes it up.

"Thank you."

No chance of ditching the slippery vegetable. The woman stands, a napkin at the ready, and watches him eat the whole thing, butter running down his fingers to congeal on his cufflinks.

"It is very good." And, to his surprise, it is.

"Now you can say you're a real Canadian."

She hangs in front of him, draws the folds of her coat around herself. He can tell this is not easy for her.

"I don't actually know many of these people. Not well."

He studies her face, a softness looking for a place to hide itself. What is it that she seems to recognize in him?

"Perhaps we could walk?"

"Yes." She answers quickly but firmly as if it were a question she'd been weighing for a very long time. "I'd like that."

MARLENE'S SHOES ARE NO more fit for walking the ravine floor than they were for square dancing. So she doesn't hesitate to take the Pole's arm when he offers it.

"My name is Tadeusz," he says, "Tadeusz Mienkiewicz. English people call me Thad."

"Nice to meet you Thad. I'm Marlene O'Halloran. Actually, I'm Irish."

"I am noticing this. Canadians never say they are Canadians. Always, they are saying 'I am Irish,' or 'I am Scottish.' Why must you always be something else than what you are?"

"I guess that's because we don't really know what that is."

"It's what I wish to become."

"Then you can tell us when you find it."

The path narrows and plunges between shoulders of sumac, and then the city is lost to them as the trail plummets into complete darkness under a stand of oaks. The wind gusts, causing the last strains of fiddle music to disappear in the static of leaves made brittle by the cold air. She remembers stories she's heard of the valley at night, the hobos who live there, bones that have been found. This is one of the city's forbidden places, but this man Thadeus navigates the dark as if it were Allen Gardens on a Sunday afternoon, telling her his sure-footedness is down to the Ukrainian mountaineers who shepherded him over the Carpathians into Hungary. At the bottom he seizes her by the waist and wheels her over the sharp drop where the path ends at some boulders on the valley floor.

"Oh! I didn't see them. I would have gone right over."

"Yes. Is good I still have night vision."

She feels a lightness spread through her whole body, as if her soul were still circling somewhere outside herself, or back at the Palace Pier jitterbugging to Louis Jordan in '43 with Fletch. But the sensation is short-lived as she lands with a start before three figures looming over a rail fence, pointed black ears pricked upwards like horns that twist in her direction.

"Don't worry it's only horses. Always, they are finding me."

Marlene is afraid of horses. A fear she can't explain. There's no traumatic incident she can remember, no near tramplings or stampedes. There are only the nightmares she had as a girl in Weston, of horses peering in at her bedroom window, teeth bared in fierce human grins, laughing at her with malicious human laughter. Nightmares that caused her to avoid the farmers' paddocks on walks home from school.

"You are frightened? Don't move too quick. That will scare them. Here, step back. They can't see you if you are too close. We make friends with this one. Look. He puts his ears to you. He is curious, wants to be your friend. If you make a friend with him they all will be your friend. He is the leader, you can tell by the way he holds his head."

Thadeus puts a hand on her waist and guides her to the horse's side. "Step here and let him see. Now ..." He lifts her hand to the animal's muzzle. "Let him smell." The soft upper lip moistens her palm, and a chuckle rolls in the horse's chest. "There now, I will show you how to be friends forever with a horse." Thadeus puts his free hand to the animal's neck, draws its head to his mouth, and blows a long deep breath into its nostrils. "This how they are saying 'hello' to each other. Now this fellow thinks I am a friendly horse."

"Where did you learn so much about horses?" Marlene asks.

"At the beginning of the war I was in the cavalry."

"You mean you were one of those ..."

"One of those men who charged the tanks?" His voice is suddenly sharp, causing the horse to strain away until he reassures it with a click of his tongue. "It was not like that."

"What was it like?"

Thadeus takes a long breath, glances into the horse's eyes, then stares into hers. "It was something that I think I am already forgetting."

Skywiper

More than anything Aleksei wanted Mitch Lobinski to take him to the place he called his "Ponderosa." He and his wife Janina went every weekend from firecracker day to Thanksgiving. When the red, rocket-shaped tail lights of their Ford Galaxie backed into the garage on Sunday nights, he ran to see what they had brought back — zinc-coloured fish swimming in steel tubs, dead rabbits that they stretched and skinned from the doorknobs in their flat upstairs. Once they even brought down a whole deer that Mitch bled from the garage rafters before butchering it with saws from his tool kit.

All Aleksei knew about Mitch's Ponderosa was that it was on an island in a place called Temagami. He imagined it looking just like the real Ponderosa on *Bonanza* — a place with big skies and fields of brown cows and prairie schooners. There would be Indians, of course, and trees that fell whenever a lumberjack shouted "Tim-ber!"

Mitch's Ponderosa was a good place to fix dogs. All winter, Mitch said he was going to take his new hunting dog Toby there in the summer and "fix him for good." Aleksei wanted to be there when that happened, but when Mitch invited him, his mother said no: too much water; too far to drive; too many accidents waiting to happen.

In the end it was Aleksei's mother who had the accident. He came home on the second last day of school and found her on the sofa with her face turned blue and her pills and empty chocolate milk glass on the coffee table. The ambulance drivers said she'd be all right after they cleaned her out and gave her a good rest. They put a rubber mask on her that looked like the guitarfish in Aleksei's *Golden Encyclopedia*, then drove her away. Aleksei thought about the one good thing this would mean. With his mother in hospital and his baby brother's sitter too full up for big kids, his Dad ,who was working all the time as usual, would have to let him go with the Lobinskis, who were leaving for their Ponderosa at the end of the week.

THEY LET HIM SIT with Toby on the narrow front seat of the boat as its iron hull bonged like a bell against amber-coloured waves. There were no cows, no prairie schooners, only giant pines twisting into the sky on a shoreline that folded and unfolded like a magic trick until Mitch steered into a wide arm of water with an island in it.

"There she is!" Mitch shouted over the engine. "My Ponderosa!"

Its real name was spelled out in white letters on the roof shingles so that bush pilots could read it from the air. As the boat came closer, Aleksei could see that the letters were cracked and speckled with moss. The lodge teetered on some boulders above the wharf and long beams had been hammered into place underneath to keep it from sliding into the lake. They carried all their supplies up to a clearing where weathered cabins sagged in the grass behind the lodge. The lodge was a dark place with long tables and a row of curtained cubicles that overlooked the water. The yellowed bodies of pikes and muskies flaked away from plaques on the wall, and a flock of deer heads hovered over the fireplace.

The dead squirrel smell disappeared as soon as Janina began to cook and, by the first evening, she had the lodge smelling like home with dill and cutlets. There was no television. Aleksei's best time in the house on Galway Avenue had been spent watching TV — when the arguments were over and his dad had gone to work evening shift at the Parish Trust, when his baby brother Blaise was already asleep, and his mother dozed in her chair after her pill and chocolate milk. That was when he'd sneak upstairs to watch *Gunsmoke* and *Wild Kingdom* and *Bat Masterson* and *The Rifleman*, sitting on the inflatable footrest with plastic roses inside, surrounded by Janina's collection of Brillo-haired dolls while Mitch ate bowl after deep-fried bowl of the smelts he had caught in the Humber River.

At Mitch's Ponderosa, all you could do at night was play chess while kerosene lamps gurgled in the rafters. Mitch told Aleksei how, in Russia, he learned to play with pieces carved out of stale bread.

"When we got too hungry," he said as he captured one of Aleksei's pawns. "We eat whole chess set. Like that." He popped the piece into his mouth and waggled it on the end of his tongue. Mitch told a lot of stories about Russia, about catching rabbits in snares made of horsehair, about hunting for mushrooms and berries, about fishing for sunfish and bullheads with his bare hands. He talked about winters so cold that when you tossed out a pail of water it would freeze before it hit the ground.

It seemed like everything to do with Mitch and Janina was because of Russia. Russia was why Janina wore a sheepskin jacket and a leather helmet, even when she stood over a hot stove. Russia was why her fingers curved in ways that fingers weren't supposed to. One night, Aleksei woke up to the sound of Toby whining and prancing in the hall. He peaked through the curtain on his cubicle and saw Mitch silvered with moonlight at a window, the dog wrapped around his knees. Seeing Aleksei, he put a finger to his lips and pointed outside.

"Listen!"

Sounds, high-pitched quavers arcing over the water.

"Wolves," Mitch whispered. "In Russia, when I was a boy, I scared to go to toilet at night because of the wolves."

His big hand fell like a wall on Aleksei's shoulder. "But this no Russia, eh Aleksei? This is Canada. Here, we are the boss!"

JANINA HAD GOT TOBY, a stubby short-haired pointer, from a friend when Mitch said he needed a dog to help with duck hunting. But he came home from his first hunt with his tail between his legs and spent the next day hiding behind furniture.

"I need dog," Mitch told Janina, "not mouse."

Since then Mitch had rescued him three times from the pound after he'd jumped the backyard fence and run off. He got a long leash attached to a runner on the clothesline, but then Toby almost hanged himself trying to escape over the fence with the leash on. That spring he got himself sprayed by a skunk and ran yelping through the house, making everything stink worse than Janina's fried onions. Neither Mitch nor Aleksei's mother could see what Toby was good for, until a night in May when Aleksei woke up crying from one of his nightmares. It was Toby who heard and who brought Janina to give him a glass of water and sing him back to sleep. After that, Mitch said that maybe he could fix Toby. He got Aleksei to borrow books about hunting dogs from the High Park library and to translate the English for him. He bought a record player with special records that had guns going pop-pop-pop underneath soft piano music. He'd play the records at meal times so that Toby would think of leftovers whenever he heard the bang of a rifle. Then Mitch bought Aleksei a little lead cap gun, a derringer, and took him and Toby to High Park.

"See, Aleksei?" Mitch explained at the big field above the duck pond. "When Toby was little somebody shoot gun, 'BANG!,' on top of his head," Mitch explained. "Now Toby's scared of big noises. That's what we gotta fix."

Aleksei played fetch and wrestled Toby in the dead leaves while Mitch fired off caps, far away at first, then coming closer until the hair went up along Toby's spine and his ears went back. After a month, Mitch could practically stand on top of them shooting caps and Toby wouldn't notice. But the real test was going to be here at Mitch's Ponderosa.

ON THE THIRD MORNING, Mitch handed Aleksei a box decorated with a lariat that was twisted to spell "Junior Marshal." Inside was a pair of six-shooters painted silver with caps, a leather belt and holsters that scratched his legs when he followed Mitch down to the wharf. Mitch ordered Toby to sit at the water's edge then waved a piece of driftwood in the air. Toby's body craned after it, as if he was attached to the stick with strings. When Mitch snapped the stick over the waves, the dog flew after it and threw up wings of spray as he landed. Once, twice, Mitch threw the stick and Toby swam back with it in his mouth. The third time, Aleksei began to fire off his caps. The six-shooters made a louder, sharper crack than the little derringer they had used in the city, but Toby just leaped higher and farther and his tail beat the water with happy strokes.

"That's good," said Mitch. "Remember, Aleksei. When something broke, always you can fix it."

"WE *FIX* YOU WE *FIX* you we *fix* you we *fix* you we *fix* you we *fix* you we *fix* you" was the chant Aleksei hummed to himself as he and Toby ran their circuit around the island each morning. Aleksei felt the pinch of muscles he never knew he had before. He ran without shoes so that the soles of his feet grew hard. He ran without clothes so that the brush scratched away the skin of his city self. He lay in the sun with Toby and grew a new skin the same iron colour as the water that cooled them at the end of their runs.

At first they kept to the shore on their runs. The interior was spooky and tense with the possibility of wild animals. Aleksei remembered the wolf calls he had heard. He reminded himself of what Mitch had told him, how it was too far for them to swim to the island and how they were the boss at his Ponderosa. But he didn't believe it until Toby began punching loops into the bush, whizzing up to the headlands and plummeting back down like an Avro Arrow breaking the sound barrier. Aleksei just had to follow and that's how he found out how safe it was on the overgrown paths that no one on the island had used in years, that led through spiny mazes of dead cedar and chambers of green buckhorn to the stone where he and Toby sacrificed ants with a magnifying glass on a cloth of gold moss. The very last path that Toby found led to the foot of the Skywiper.

It was the tallest tree on the island, screwing its way into the air over the clearing at the island's north tip. Aleksei called it the Skywiper because of the way it poked through the roof of the forest and swayed as if it was wiping its way through to the stars. It was perfect for climbing, with branches that began at the ground and sprouted straight out from the trunk like rungs every couple of feet, and it reminded Aleksei of the idea that had stuck in his head when he was watching the snakes.

The only animals on the island were the garter snakes that lived in the long grass near the lodge. Mitch showed him how to tromp through the grass the way he said the British had taught him to do in Persia to protect against vipers. "But these are no viper," he said. "They eating mice, frogs, bugs. They good snakes." At midday the garter snakes sunned themselves on the boulders and hunted frogs. Aleksei had studied how they lifted themselves into the air with frog legs windmilling between their unhinged jaws. Seeing the frogs slip down their gullets to make twitchy black bumps in their middles, he imagined how good it would be if he could swallow Mitch's Ponderosa just like that, carry it around alive inside of himself, like a secret power.

When he looked up the long telescope of the Skywiper's trunk, Aleksei pretended how, at the very top of the tree, he could drink the whole island in through his eyes. He tried to climb the Skywiper on the day he found it, but its limbs danced away from his feet and even the heavy trunk began to swim in his arms at a point just below the forest ceiling, where the thick ribs of its bark turned silvery and smooth. Aleksei started to measure his time at Mitch's Ponderosa in branches. Each day he climbed a little higher into the gold-green flux of the Skywiper's needles, picking his way among cones that sparkled with beads of clear sap. At the end of the third week he got to the branches just below the forest canopy. He knew every lobe of fungus, every vein of rusty gum and he came down from the tree, sticky and flecked with bark, to lie in the clearing and giggle while Toby licked him clean.

THEY WENT FISHING AT dawn and at sunset every day. Mitch taught Aleksei about the baits, spoons, and spinners you needed to catch pike and took him to the places he had learned about from the Indians, smaller lakes you had to reach by portage. Mitch kept boats hidden on the shores of these lakes so that he only had to carry the motor that looked like a scaly sea beast dripping seaweed down his back. In the hours that they sat waiting for a bite, Mitch told Aleksei how, at the battle of Monte Cassino, he and his platoon had carried anti-tank guns up the cliffs piece by piece then put them back together to fire point blank at the Germans. He told Aleksei how he had walked out of Siberia in snow up to his middle to join the British in Persia. He talked about a place called Palestine where he learned to ride camels. Then Italy, then Canada, where he met Aleksei's dad on a beet farm in Manitoba.

"You daddy, Tadeusz Mienkiewicz, is good man, Aleksei. Always helping mens to find job. Getting mens money to start business. Maybe you daddy is too good. But you don't listen what you mammy say. When you mammy talking like that about you daddy, is talkin' pills."

Mitch spat the word into the bottom of the boat.

"After you baby brother come, the doctors they give you mammy pills to make happy. Pills to make sleep. Pills for this, pills for that. She take and take. They makin' her crazy, those pills, and now she can't stop and that's why she go to hospital. You understand me, Aleksei?"

Aleksei stared at the place among the tackle boxes where Mitch had spat his words and remembered his mother's pills scattered across the carpet. Her face under the fins of the oxygen mask.

"You don't worry, Aleksei," Mitch said. "We fix it up. We soldiers, yeah? We do what we gotta do."

ALEKSEI WOKE UP WITH dog breath in his face and Toby's black nose an inch from his own on the pillow. To get there the dog had stepped over the plank that lay flat across the doorway to keep him out. Toby had always been afraid of planks. Back in the city, Janina had put one across her kitchen doorway after she had caught him eating the garbage. The first time he tried to jump over it, it fell with a "BANG!" and he had run yelping down the hall. Ever since then, all she had to do to keep him out of a place was lay a plank flat on the floor.

Now that Toby had lost his fear of planks, Mitch said he was ready for "the big step."

Mitch came down to the wharf that afternoon with his eyebrows stitched up under the peak of his green hunting cap and a shotgun cocked open over the crook of his arm.

"Find stick," he grunted as he slipped two shells into the breech.

Aleksei found a stick he was sure Toby would like, bone-shaped, with big knots at each end. Mitch snapped shut the barrel and gestured at the water.

"Okay, you play with him," he said as he mounted the stairs and disappeared up the forest path.

Aleksei wheeled the stick in the air until Toby danced underneath it as if he were attached to it with strings. Then Aleksei spun the stick over the water and the dog sailed after it, seized it in his teeth, and swam back. Toby fetched and fetched until the first shot sounded far back in the woods, the first real gunshot Aleksei had ever heard.

The sound of it smacked against his cheek. Toby yelped, lost the stick, retrieved it, and paddled to the dock. The second shot came nearer and louder, when Toby was back on the wharf. He jumped straight up and came down with his legs in a tangle, but Aleksei got him interested in the stick again and he plunged after it. The shots started coming faster and louder. Toby thrashed and sank, came up coughing, circled, not sure what to do. Finally, spluttering and stickless, he paddled to the dock. But he was too weak and confused to pull himself out of the water. Aleksei knelt and hooked his fingers under the dog's collar. Just as he was pulling Toby out, Mitch fired his gun on the other side of the lodge. The dog leaped with a howl back into the water taking Aleksei with him. Claws tore at his face and clothes and pushed him toward the weedy bottom. Then something yanked from above and he was on the dock with Mitch's fist knotted in his shirt. Toby flopped on the planking next to him with his jaws working, like a big hairy fish.

Mitch shook his head at the retching animal.

"What I'm gonna do?" he asked the squadron of clouds that shipped eastward over the choppy water. "How we gonna fix this crazy dog?"

That night Aleksei heard Janina and Mitch arguing in Polish after he'd gone to bed, their voices thrusting Toby's name at each other under the hiss of the kerosene.

MITCH PUT A WOODEN crate in the meadow outside the lodge and cut a door into it. This was Toby's new home. Mitch said living outside would toughen him up. From now on Toby was a working dog, but Aleksei didn't see him doing much work. The dog spent most of the day chained to a stake in the meadow while Mitch sawed and chopped his way through cord after cord of firewood, as if the man were trying to set some kind of an example for the dog. He dragged the rusty propane cylinders that lay in the long grass like unexploded shells down to the wharf for the propane barge to pick up. He spent hours propping up the old cabins and all the other things that were falling down around the lodge. They had to be ready for duck hunting, he said, and time was running out.

Once a day, Mitch took the dog and his shotgun to the north clearing for practice. Aleksei wasn't allowed to go. He had to stay inside with Janina who lost herself in making him fritters and pierogies and *pączki* doughnuts as if the splatter of deep-fried doughy things sizzling and bubbling would cover up the gunshots and howls that blew back through the trees. She said that Toby would be fixed up soon. But Aleksei knew that something was going on and nobody wanted to put a name on it.

There were fewer fishing trips and only at sunset to spots on the big lake. Mitch didn't sit next to Aleksei on the middle seat, the way he had before. He stayed bunched up by the motor and talked to the night about his plans for the lodge.

"When you live like me and your daddy lived," he said, "you got to have that place you carry in your head. That place where nobody touch you. That's my Ponderosa."

Mitch talked about his own father who had been a forester in the marshes that he said were just like the land around Temagami, except without the rocks. He talked about how princes would come from Warsaw and from Moscow to hunt ducks and wild boar with his father and grandfather. He said that knowing the forest had made his family powerful. That was why they had been the first to be taken when the Russians arrived.

"I lose my daddy. I lose my mammy, sisters, brothers. I lose my whole country, just like you daddy," he said. "But look at the forest we got in Canada. Plenty ducks, deer, bear, lotsa fish. I make everything like before."

Mitch kept saying how important it was to bring the bosses from the mill to his Ponderosa, the same way important people had come to hunt with his family in Poland. Aleksei knew these bosses. Janina fogged up her kitchen with lilac spray whenever they came to plan their deer hunts with Mitch. They wore fedora hats with feathers in the bands and carried bottles wrapped in brown paper. The bosses called Aleksei "kiddo," and they invented the name "Mitch" for Mitch, because Mieczysław was too hard for them to say. Mitch said they had made him a "little boss" at the mill because of the deer hunt and they would make him a "big boss" if he took them hunting for ducks. He said he needed a good hunting dog for the duck hunting. He didn't say anything about Toby.

ON THE FIRST MORNING of the last weekend, Mitch took two guns up the forest path — the shotgun plus the rifle he said he kept for "nuisances" — and Aleksei didn't believe that Janina was crying because of onions. If he really wanted to know anything about anything, he would have to go see for himself. When the sound of the shotgun began wafting back through the forest, he hid among the bags and trunks that Janina had packed for the trip home. Then he slipped out the door and ran for the Skywiper.

"We*fix*youwe*fix*youwe*fix*youwe*fix*youwe*fix*youwe*fix*youwe*fix*you." The chant was just a sound that kept him steady, like saying the Latin at church. Coming over the heights, he heard squiggles of Toby noise between the shots. The smell of gunpowder scratched his nose as he approached the clearing. It would be easy for a stray shot to blast through the screen of shrubs around the clearing, but he would be safe in the Skywiper. So he ran to the tree and climbed, past the place where the bark smoothed out, feeling the trunk grow thin between his knees. He passed over the branches he had conquered until he broke through the forest roof and the tree held him swinging in the wind.

Through a veil of blue smoke, he could see the ground glittering with spilt ammunition and Toby all teeth and foam at the end of his chain. The shotgun was on the ground, cocked open like a broken body. Mitch had the rifle to his shoulder. His shirt tails were out, a big sweaty blotch spreading down his back as he aimed for the white star on Toby's chest. Aleksei wanted to shout down for Mitch to stop, but the wind sucked the breath out of him as the Skywiper pitched from side to side.

The shot never came. Mitch stood there squinting down the barrel of the rifle, as if he knew all along that Janina, who had followed Aleksei the minute she saw he was gone, would edge up to him in her leather helmet and sheepskin, would ease the gun out of his hands with her bent fingers and let him slump into her arms.

Aleksei stayed invisible up in the Skywiper. He saw the hills plunging into forever as a million miles of soft air pushed over his skin. Coiled around the Skywiper's tip, he could see every inch of the island and the deep water that protected it from bears and wolves and wildcats. He opened his eyes, swallowed the island whole. He was in the place that Mitch had talked about, the place where no one could touch him. Nothing else mattered.

An Offering

A white cross falls out of a burning sky. Its arms unravel, then it wallops into her and she is awake and staring at the red sumac licking her bedroom window.

Work. That's what chases dreams from her head. After her Fredryku has dressed, eaten and left for the mill, she puts on a house dress printed with yellow daisies and crosses the street to bring in the garbage cans for blind Mrs. Wright. She goes next door to feed the cat at the Rajcas, who are in Chicago at a funeral. Then she does all the chopping for a soup she wants to make for Pan Solecki, whose wife is in the hospital.

Before the children arrive, she sits down to some tea and stale honey cake. Her fingers wander to the lump in her neck. She feels it bobbing at her collarbone when she swallows, laughs, or coughs. It's best to forget about the lump, but before she can forget she has to remember not to forget her appointment. Next Tuesday she will finally see the doctor who knows what to say about her lump. She must-must-must remember to tell the parents to pick their children up early.

Another call from the Grafstein woman. To see if there is any change.

"No change," says Borżena. "I have already six children coming. Is too much."

She hangs up, looks to the Black Madonna of Częstochowa hanging over the kitchen table and asks forgiveness. The mannish little Jesus on the Madonna's arm lifts two fingers in a blessing, but there is no absolution in the *Matka Boska*'s narrow eyes.

Now the children come. First, as always, Blaise, or rather his father, Pan Mienkiewicz, with a face hanging like a dishrag.

"Where is Blaise?" she asks.

"On. Your. Lawn."

Four-year-old Blaise rolls in the fallen leaves. Before she can tell Pan Mienkiewicz about the early pickup on Tuesday he's halfway down the street.

The TV keeps Blaise quiet until Borzena sees Autumn and Zooey coming up the walk. She turns the TV off. Television is on a long list of things that Autumn and Zooey are not allowed to see, do, and eat. The girls creep in behind their mother, who is one of these beatniks she has been hearing about, always wearing black sweaters and pants that match the hair that falls all the way to her waist.

"Bojayna," says the mother. "Wonderful news! A job interview. Next Tuesday night at six o'clock. You'll have to keep the girls late."

This a good thing. If the girls' mother gets a job, maybe she can start to pay for the babysitting. So Borzena says nothing about the doctor. Ryku is on the day shift. He can look after the girls when he gets home. She turns the TV back on as soon as the woman is gone. It stays on while she puts in a load of laundry and mops the kitchen floor before the babies arrive. She checks diapers and sends the older ones to the bathroom. Blaise stands with his pants to his ankles, a proud smirk on his lips and a perfectly formed turd at his feet. How, she wonders, could this be the younger brother of Aleksei Mienkiewicz, who was such a good boy, a prince like his father.

At mid-morning Borzena rakes up a new pile of leaves on the front lawn. The children burrow into them and then leap out like flames in their brightly coloured coats. Blaise beats little Zooey with a stick.

"Blaise, what you do?"

She pries the stick from the boy's fingers and sits him on the porch steps.

"Mrs. Sigalski?"

A short, big-eyed woman smiles nervously from the foot of the walk.

"We were just walking past and I thought I would stop to introduce ourselves. I'm Ruth Grafstein and this," she says, "is Jacob."

The Grafstein woman hoists a red-haired boy out of his stroller. Borzena feels a thump in her chest.

"Are you all right?" says the Grafstein woman.

UNTIL THE VOYTYLO FAMILY trudged into Karstwo in the summer of 1941, no one in Borzena's home village had seen such red hair, a thick, luxurious fall of it on twelve-year-old Danuta, wild mops like the burning bush on Nikolai and little Magda.

"For sure they are Jews," said Borzena's father. "Who else could have such hair?"

But the Voytylos were supposed to be cousins of Tomczak, the village reeve who was certainly not a Jew. They arrived in between the Russian retreat and the German advance, dragging a cart stacked high with trunks and boxes. Tomczak arranged for them to take the house next door to Borzena's family. It had sat empty ever since the Russians deported the village schoolteacher.

"Eh, Tomczak," people asked, "what are these cousins of yours?"

Tomczak looked at the ground, spat and said, "They are on their own. That's what they are."

After the massacre at Baranica, just a couple of miles across the marshes, everyone became nervous. It was not a good time to be different and everything about the Voytylos was different. That hair, the faces that shone blue with hunger. Borzena remembers Pan Voytylo's hands floating around him whenever he spoke, as if they were made of goose down, soft and pale and completely unlike the earth-blackened hands of everyone else in Karstwo.

"Look at him!" her father scoffed as he stood at the kitchen window watching Voytylo fumble with some mouldy seed potatoes in his garden. "What kind of a man is this who can't even plant?"

The Voytylos weren't prepared for their first winter. Their provisions ran out soon after Christmas and Pan Voytylo was seen trudging around the village wrapped in blankets, begging scraps. He didn't get much. The villagers had seen the cart stacked high with trunks and boxes when the family arrived. They were hiding valuables for sure — gold, silver, maybe diamonds that they should have offered for barter.

Borzena's mother slipped morsels of food to the family without her father knowing, using tricks to make a little extra soup or to stretch the flour just a little further so that there would be a few dumplings to spare.

"You are our little mother," Pan Voytylo said to Borzena one evening as he watched Magda, their youngest, greedily sucking at the soup she had brought. "You give us life with this food."

When they learned that Pani Voytylo was pregnant, other women sent food and extra clothes for the children. When spring came the men gave seeds for cabbage and tomatoes and cucumbers and they helped Voytylo expand his garden plots so that there would be enough food for the next winter.

Borzena's father refused to help. "The Germans are shooting people just for looking at people like that," he said, "and soon there will be lots of people ready to turn that Voytylo, and everyone who helps him, over to the SS for a crust of bread. It's bad enough we have to live next door to him."

And when Pan Voytylo began giving lessons in exchange for the villagers' help, Borzena's father refused to let her go. She wasn't allowed to play with the Voytylo children either, but they had become friends during her winter visits. Borzena had told them the local stories like the one about Stara Nadzieja, the witch who, in the time of the Tsars, made all the cows in Karstwo walk on the walls of the landowners' barns. Then the boy, Nikolai, pretended to say the mass in Latin using a tin cup for a chalice and a heel of stale bread for the host. He had been an altar boy at the cathedral in Lwów and everyone said what a fine priest he would make one day.

The Voytylos told her about Lwów, the tall buildings and the automobiles and the ballet and the theatre for children. Danuta told her about the books she had read from England and America, about Alice's Wonderful Land and the Little Women of Louisa May Alcott.

Anne of Green Gables was Danuta's favourite book. In the summer the children met secretly in the forest, in spite of their parents' warning about the partisans. Danuta named the forest Avonlea and called the crayfish pond "Lake of Shining Waters." She said the forester's path was a "Lover's Lane" and made the other children gather gooseberries for "Strawberry Socials." In the clearings she recited whole speeches that ended with her holding up the braids that Borzena had woven in her hair and saying, "Oh Diana, my red hair is an absolute curse!"

The Voytylos' baby was born at the height of summer, a girl who had the same pale skin and blue eyes as her sisters and brother, and the same thatch of hair red as sunset. They called her Jadwiga. With Mrs. Voytylo absorbed in the baby, four-year-old Magda found herself displaced and attached herself to Borzena whenever she could, knotting a little fist in the skirts of her "little mother" and following her around the house with a thumb thrust in her mouth.

Magda seldom spoke and never laughed. When the Voytylos first came to Karstwo, Danuta and Nikolai said that Magda had been like this ever since the soldiers had come to their house in Lwów. But the family was overjoyed to see her smile when Borzena gave her one of the little dolls that she had learned to weave from sheaves of grass. From then on they would bring Magda to her every time she entered the house, as if for a blessing.

Still the rumour persisted that the Voytylos were Jews who paid Tomczak money to say they were his cousins. Borzena knew that it wasn't true. She had seen the icon of the *Matka Boska* the family had made with a picture torn from a book. She said the rosary with them on the feast of the Assumption. She had heard how well Nikolai said the mass.

Borzena's father laughed when she told him these things.

"They're clever, those Jews," he said. "They become whatever they have to so they can get whatever they want."

THE BABIES ARRIVE IN the late morning, and Borzena sets them down in the playpen so that she can feed the children cheese pierogi. Autumn and Zooey are not supposed to have pierogi. Their mother says they have too many "glootums." But the girls lick the butter from their fingers and ask for more. So do the others after Blaise steals the last of their portions. For this Borzena makes him sit on a stool beside the refrigerator while she feeds the babies their pablum and the older children eat *kompot* and poppyseed cake from Wysotska's bakery.

At nap time she spreads the children through the house to keep them from waking one another. Blaise is too old to nap but naps are the only way Borzena gets to eat so she puts him on the living room couch where he must pretend to sleep while she watches him. There's no telling what he could get up to, like the time he found an old wall plug with the bare wires attached. Borzena heard the crackling sound and ran down to Ryku's workshop to find him gaping at the white flames that spat from the socket where he had plugged in the cord.

Blaise thrashes on the couch while she eats some rye bread and a little chicken soup. As she swallows, she feels the lump. It bobs under her fingertips, playing hide and seek among the tendons of her neck. It began the same way bad things begin on *General Hospital*, with the doctor pressing his thumb at a place above her collarbone and saying, "It's probably nothing."

But what if it's not nothing? Who will look after her Ryku? Who will look after these children? Who will keep spare keys for her neighbours? Or bring in the garbage cans for Mrs. Wright?

Too much thinking. There's just enough nap time left to iron the linen. She takes the hamper from the dining room table. Blaise hums to himself on the couch. If he sees her moving around, that's the end of it. She creeps back toward the kitchen, but, in a moment's weakness, she stops at the sideboard to look at the photo of a fine red-haired woman cradling a newborn. The photo is her answer to all those who think it is a shame she and Ryku never had children of their own. Strangers to the house, repairmen, election workers, mistake them for her daughter and grandchild. She doesn't correct them.

Blaise bounces on the sofa and shouts, "I'm awake now! I'm awake now!" Borzena drops the hamper and whisks him into the kitchen before he can wake the others.

She decides to make cookies, takes out the flour, sugar, and food colouring, then pulls a step stool to the counter for the boy. She measures out the ingredients and he churns them into dough. Then she lets him roll the dough flat on the cutting board. Borzena has never seen him so quiet.

"Now Blaise, we make Halloween!"

She gives him the cutters shaped like pumpkins and witch cats. "What you think? Maybe you be baker man when you grow?"

Blaise smiles sweetly and tells her to shut up. Borzena laughs. Blaise is Blaise. She won't spoil the moment. How often does he do something like this at home? He should be home with his mother, but she is sick again. She is sick so often. Borzena doesn't understand these Canadian women. How can they be sick so much when their lives are so good? A shame that Pan Mienkiewicz didn't find a good strong Polish girl to help him in his work.

Outside the kitchen window and across the back fences, the red maples rise like a picture from another of her dreams, one she's been having ever since her first autumn in this country: trees growing inside houses, black limbs unfurling through the windows, the houses roofed in crimson leaf.

THE GERMANS GREW WILD as the Russian counterattack approached, like animals before a storm. There were ambushes. A mine blew off the leg of a young soldier just a kilometre up the road. Borzena remembers them carrying him past their house on a stretcher, whinnying like a colt and hugging the severed limb to his chest.

When a sentry got his throat cut at a nearby supply dump, the Germans brought in the SS.

The SS soldiers were nothing like the killers they had heard about. They were boys who barely filled their uniforms, marching alongside a dented staff car that carried a captain who sat buried in his greatcoat like an old woman under a shawl. On the day of their arrival they ran from house to house pounding on doors with their rifle butts and shouting, "*Raus, raus*." Borzena's insides turned to stew as the soldiers herded everyone to the dirt square in front of the village hall.

The captain stood in the open car and flicked a pair of leather gloves across his chest, tips missing from three of the fingers. Schulz, the *volksdeutsch* from Baranica, stood rigid by the car, twisting his cap in his hands as he translated the captain's words.

"Partisans do not live on air," he said. "They need help." The villagers would be wise to help the Reich by revealing the spies among them. Otherwise his soldiers would conduct their own investigations.

Borzena pretended to sleep as her parents argued.

"You have no proof," her mother said.

"The Germans don't want proof," her father answered. "They want an offering."

Borzena's family stayed in their beds that night as shrieks, gunshots, and soldiers' laughter rose from the far side of the village. The SS had begun their investigations. In the morning, word passed that four houses had been "inspected." They had murdered Hubal's youngest, a boy three years old, by throwing him against the side of a barn until he died.

"Well," said Borzena's father. "And now we know what we must do."

The following day Borzena woke to a rumble of motors, the squeal of brakes and to soldiers clanking and thundering in the road out front of their house. By the time she was fully awake and able to look out her window, the Germans had the Voytylo house surrounded, the soldiers rigid in their positions. Inside the house, she could hear Jadwiga, the baby, crying.

Borzena's father burst through the door and told his family to get down and keep still. But Borzena stayed by the back window where she could watch.

In the Voytylo's garden, Pan Voytylo and the German captain stared at each other down the length of the front path. Voytylo stood with his arms spread across the door, barring the way. The Captain flicked his gloves at the garden gate as the *volksdeutsch* Schulz translated his orders for Voytylo to move aside.

"*Idiota!*" hissed Borzena's father. "Why doesn't he give himself up?"

Two of the young soldiers tried to seize him, but Voytylo drove them back. Finally, a sergeant knocked him to the ground with his rifle. They tied Voytylo by his hands and feet. Then they kicked at him until his white sleeping shirt was dark with his blood and the filth from their boots. Pani Voytylo stood in the open door with the baby at her shoulder, held back by two sentries. They dragged her husband to the gate and stood him with his back to the road.

"Not like this!" Borzena's father said, squeezing out the words as if someone had placed a millstone on his chest. "Not in front of his children."

BORZENA SLIDES THE TRAYS of Halloween cookies into the oven and soon the air thickens with their scent. Blaise helps her wash the cutters in a bowl of warm water and together they watch the shapes disappear in the cloudy liquid.

This Halloween business is so strange. Pumpkins, costumes, tricks and treats are all very lovely for the children, but who goes to the cemetery to light a candle for the dead? She would be so happy if there were some place to go and say a prayer for the dead and light candles on All Souls. But Borzena's dead have no resting place. They follow her around this house, crowding her thoughts, stoking her imagination so that Little Magda curls up in the sewing room with Autumn and Zooey while Nikolai fills the hollow Blaise has left in the sofa and the memory of Danuta follows Borzena around the kitchen like a pack of worries.

"Phone that Grafstein woman!" she hears the command in the exact tone Danuta would have used, chattering like a lark. "Call the mother of that red-haired boy! You must! You must!"

When the cookies are done, Borzena puts them out to cool. She gives a pumpkin-shaped one to Blaise. She asks the *Matka Boska* to forgive her. Then she takes one for herself.

THE CAPTAIN STEPPED UP behind Pan Voytylo, tapped him on each shoulder as if to bless him with the fingerless gloves. Voytylo looked at the sky, lips working, prepared to die, but not for what happened next.

The captain gestured and stepped back. The front door slammed shut on Pani Voytylo and the soldiers at the side of the house produced bottles stuffed with rags. They set fire to the rags and tossed the bottles through the windows. The bottles gave a cheerful pop and flared inside the building.

Mrs. Voytylo's screams escaped over the window sills on black branches of smoke. Borzena heard Danuta's voice crying "Tata! Tata! Help us! Someone!"

Borzena's father staggered back from the window. "The children," he stammered. "His wife! I didn't think. Who could know they would do such a thing?"

Borzena ran for the door, her father protesting feebly after her.

"I did it for us, Borzena. We would have been next, don't you see?"

She reached the fence at the side of the house just as the shooting started. The air was full of what looked like little black birds, wings tipped with flame. Papers, books. That's what had filled the boxes and trunks Pan Voytylo had dragged all the way from Lwów. Now they made the house burn all the more fiercely.

Nikolai Voytylo's choking black figure leapt from a window at the side of the house. A soldier fired a burst and the boy turned in the air and landed in his father's garden, his body twisted like a fallen scarecrow. Danuta burst through the front door and started to run toward her father. Her braids stood straight up as another soldier fired and she dissolved in a red mist.

The soldiers laughed at Voytylo's efforts to reach Danuta on his bound legs. They knocked him down and he tried to squirm toward her, howling her name through broken teeth.

Borzena eased herself over the fence and stepped past the soldiers. Something drew her to the loft window at the side of the house. She had no idea of what was about to happen, but she had never been so certain of what she was supposed to do. She walked past without even flinching as the captain shot Pan Voytylo in the back of the head, feeling a perfect calm that she has since known only in her dream of the falling cross. Afterwards no one believed that Magda was the one waiting for her there. But Borzena remembers Magda's puzzled face appearing out of the black smoke, her features white as the blanket swaddling the baby on her shoulder.

Deaf to the shouts of the Germans, Borzena stepped forward, and cried "Magda! I'm here. Jump. To me!"

Magda's hands shot up and Jadwiga took flight, the fine curls flickering like rose petals in the wind, the blanket unwinding from her shoulders like the arms of the crucifix. This was the cross the

Matka Boska had chosen for her. She would carry it forever. Gladly. There seemed no end to how wide Borzena's arms could open.

FREDRYKU PHONES AT TWO-THIRTY to tell Borzena he's been moved to the afternoon shift. He will have to work late every day for the next week, including Tuesday. She doesn't tell him about the doctor with the answers. Work comes first. The answers will just have to wait.

The phone call has woken the girls upstairs. On her way up to get them, Borzena stops for another look at the photograph on the sideboard. How beautiful Jadwiga has grown up to be, twenty years old, married to a medical student in Poznan, and already a little mother herself. The baby is such an angel, she should have wings! Borzena would love to go to Poland in a year or two, just to hear the child call her *babcia*. But that privilege belongs to the aunt from Łódź who took Jadwiga from her after the war. After that, there was nothing left in Karstwo for Borzena, only the voice of Danuta whispering in the pines along Lovers' Lane and the reeds of the Lake of Shining Waters. That voice has followed her here, to the country of *Anne of Green Gables*, and it speaks to her through the long days alone in this house, with only the children for company.

"Pleasepleasepleaseplease call the mother of the red-haired boy," it says. "You must! You must! You must!"

"I will," Borzena says aloud as she starts up the stairs.

The Source

Patrol boats strafe the sidewalks. Clanking half-tracks prowl the streetcar lines and the traffic roars like D-Day. From the cover of a parked Studebaker, Blaise figures the situation. Ricky Dyzbanuzyk had hockey, Andy Jáworski had altar boy practice, and his big brother Alex said this whole idea was just stupid. So as far as Blaise is concerned they're all dead in a blasted barge on Sunnyside Beach. He's on his own and the commandos of the National Rescue Patrol wait for him across the road in High Park.

Blaise adjusts the National Rescue Patrol insignia he has drawn with crayons on a chunk of old bed sheet and pinned to his sleeve. It has two bars, green and blue for land and sea, with crossed rifles and anchors in the middle. He checks his Johnny Seven combination Tommy gun, machine pistol, and grenade launcher. He tightens the strap on his Monkey Division helmet and checks his plastic Navy Seals watch.

It's been at least an hour since Blaise snuck out of the house instead of doing piano. His father, or someone, will be after him.

He runs for it, zigzagging through the traffic then bounding down into the park. At the shore of the duck pond he hits the dirt and his imaginary commandos — Little John, Kirk, Frenchie, and Sarge — gather themselves out of the muck. They know their mission: guide the PT 109 north to the Source of the pond's water.

Blaise takes his brother's scale model PT boat out of his backpack. All that's left of its crew are plastic feet anchored in islands of dried glue along the deck. Most of its bristly bits — masts, guns, antennae — are snapped off, but there's still a flagpole at the bow, perfect for tying on string. He knots on a length of it to guide the 109 upstream. Frenchie, Little John, Kirk, and Sarge want to know why they have to make the trip so extra hard for themselves by dragging a stupid boat. Blaise says it's because that's what the National Rescue Patrol is there to do: hard things.

He makes a quick genuflection by the water and launches the 109. It wobbles up the surface, looking just like the movie with Cliff Robertson. The patrol creeps up the pathless shore, pulling the 109 behind it and resisting the temptation to look for toads in the leafy rot or to search for the eggs of dive-bombing swans.

They come to a slippery bit at the bottom of some cliffs.

"Heads up palookas and watch out for landslides," Blaise warns his men. "They'll sweep you right into the murk." Blaise knows what's down under the water. That Chinese pagoda listing in the pond's middle is in fact the superstructure of the battleship *Arizona*, sunk there by Japanese zeroes to block their way. That water is a trap made of subcaverns for gorgly demons. It's haunted by the ghosts of Grenadiers who once upon a time were lured onto the pond's thin ice by Indians and fell through under the weight of their heavy gear. The Grenadiers are still down there, undead and manoeuvring in full regalia.

The National Rescue Patrol tows the 109 into the channel that links the duck pond with the hockey pond. Before the ice went, Blaise skated on these Grenadier-gobbling lagoons with Maple Leafs who smelt of wet leather and Vitalis. He prays to the saving soul of Johnny Bower and the swift spirit of Frank Mahovlich to guide him to the Source. Blaise admires the 109's easy passage between the titanic ice blobs that still float just off the shore, but then he imagines trouble in the ranks. Kirk, the new kid, tries to make mutiny. *"Oh sir, why don't we just blow the boat up and say we didn't. We gots cherry bombs, lighter fluid, and matches. Let's reduce this tub to flaming goo!"*

Blaise says what has to be done.

"Sarge?"

"Sir?"

"Shoot 'em."

And it's done.

They're at the top of the hockey pond, where the creek flows down from the Source. The National Rescue Patrol keeps to the brushy side of the water, invisible from the paved shore where car-coated dads and their woolly children feed ducks. It hasn't been long since Blaise was one of those kids. Now they're all suspects, collaborators with the constable who goes from dad to dad with an open notebook.

"Ten years old," he hears the jackbooted officer say as he holds up a description. "The boy disappeared two hours ago, covered in toy army gear."

"Krauts, men," Blaise whispers. *"Run for it."*

No one sees the patrol slip into a culvert that carries the Source-bound creek under the road. There's someone in it: a teenager — spotty-faced, smoking, f-word using — in buckskins and a Yankees ballcap.

"'Zat you those cops're lookin' for, kid?"

"Mebbe," Blaise answers, making himself big with a sneer.

"Better you than me'z all I can say. Hey, cool gear you got on. What's yer badge say?"

"National Rescue Patrol."

"Oh yeah? Watcha gonna rescue? Ants?"

One flip of a grenade frags the teenager into dog meat and the National Rescue Patrol makes a break for it up the creek shore, the 109 planing alongside them. They scuttle past a bunker disguised as a peanut vendor's shed, past the playground with its tyrannosauric twists of painted iron. Hills rise like fortress walls on either side of the creek. He feels the closeness of the Source. It will be somewhere near Bloor Street, farther than Julie, Tony, Ricky Dizbanuzyk, or any National Rescue Patrolman has ever been. When he tells how he cracked the secret of the Source, they'll puke.

The trees are leafless. Their branches tangle the sky like streetcar wire.

"Look out, men. Dog pooh!" Jerry has mined the path with the stuff. Coils of it have been set in amazing colours — brick red, chalk white, and explosion yellow — so it's impossible to hit the dirt when cover is called for.

But they've got to take cover. Now. Up the valley road comes a cop car, purring like a Leopard tank. Blaise imagines its burpgunshots blatting all around him.

"I'm hit! I'm hit!" Sarge squawls and disappears in the muck.

Blaise runs with the 109 bucking on its line. The cop car gets close enough that he can hear the spit of its radio but then it U-turns and rumbles back toward the pond. Blaise sits on a stump and breathes in the sweet park smell of wood chips and rotting oak leaves. Bare shrubs make boneyards of the slopes. He can see right through them to where heaps from the animal pens steam and stink.

"Never mind, kid," a voice cries out. "In the filth is the beginning of our putrefaction."

Oh swinging sticks of Tim Horton, Blaise thinks, *it's Inkman.*

The tramp rises out of the sludge and skitters down the bank. Inkman is the ultimate not-to-be-spoken-to stranger. Blaise has seen him a thousand times on Copernicus Avenue — picking through garbages, faking leglessness in front of Loblaws and selling pencils. He's got on his Leafs toque with little cloth Detroit Red Wings pinned and flapping on either side of his head. Snakes of hair spill down the shoulders of his torn parka. He squints in the direction where the police car went. "They lookin' fr' you, kid?"

Blaise nods.

"Runned away. En'cha?"

Blaise nods.

"Wha' for? They beatin' yuh?"

Blaise shakes his head and points to the creek. "I'm findin' the Source."

"Ah-ha! Well, that's a bizarre mystery and a worthy pursuit."

Then Inkman squats prayerfully beside the bobbling PT 109.

"Well, well, well," he says. "Whadda we got here? Motor Torpedo Boat, an ELCO 80-footer by the looks of her."

"She had 1350 horsepower engines," says Blaise.

"Yep, she could cruise at forty-three knots. I know the boats. Served on 'em." Inkman whips himself to attention and salutes. "Ordinary seaman, 4th Patrol Torpedo Flotilla, Aleutians, '44 and '45."

He takes the model in hand and carves a wake into the water's surface. "Those were the years," he says. "Then the war was over. We beached our boats outside Nanaimo and torched 'em. Fire and water. Story of my life. Howzbout a slug of maiden's milk?"

He offers a bottle. Blaise shakes his head no.

"Not quite ready fer the deep elixir, eh? You better glean your own way, buster. But remember. These are my woods and I'll be watching."

Inkman hops back up through wavy ribs of sumac and disappears at the top of the bank.

Blaise calls what's left of the National Rescue Patrol up from the slime where they've been hiding, unhitches the 109, and plucks his way onwards.

The current is strong and it knocks the boat every which way — a sure sign that the Source is near. Blaise tries to imagine it: a place of glassy waters sparkling with secrets, the beginnings of everything. But first there are obstacles. Blaise jigs the 109 around a shopping cart scuttled across the stream. Then he makes her leap like a salmon over a tiny waterfall.

The creek widens and it gets hard to know where the water ends and the shore begins. The valley is a bog that slurps into his desert boots and makes worms of his toes. There are dead things the snow has left behind, furry smears with paws stretched out on the rocks, guts spilt like dark jam. The arse end of a dead squirrel, bloated big as a dog's, sticks out of the bank.

One by one his patrolmen get caught in the bogs and sink from his sight. There are no lifesavers, no inflatables. He'll have to face the Source alone. Everyone at National Rescue Patrol headquarters will think he has perished with his men. He imagines the talk in the ops room. *"And are they gone then?"* asks the adjutant with a swish of his swaggerstick. *"The whole squadron?"*

"Tommyrot," blurts back the Wing Commander. *"You cawn't kill a squaw-drun!"*

Then, for no reason at all, Blaise feels something he's never felt before on a mission: he feels fake. The teenager under the bridge was right. There's nothing to rescue here. His shoulders sink under the dumb weight of the pillows that wad his backpack and he thinks about Ricky and Tony and Andy doing ordinary things. Maybe it would be better to be ordinary — dry, warm, safe. But how can you live without a secret like the Source?

It's all at stake now, all his imaginings. He forges forward but looks backwards. A line of police come round a bend in the road. They kick every clod and whack at stands of petrified milkweed. The yellow cruiser creeps behind them.

"Whisssshhht. Hey kid. Getyerassuphere!"

It's Inkman, waving a snaky branch on the bank top, making an invitation to stink. Blaise can't resist. He ties the 109 to a gnarled root, tosses a hunk of brush over it, and clambers up to where Inkman squats in a foxhole.

"Down, kid, down," he says through a jowl of mushy teeth. Blaise feels cold muck press through his woollies.

Inkman leads him to a teepee made of branches and sealed with "leaves and earth. He lifts a burlap flap and waves Blaise through to an inside floored with Cola signs and licence plates. The walls are papered with naked women and holy calendars purpled with the days of Lent. In the middle, a church's worth of candles circle a fire pit. Inkman opens a tin of butts and licks together a smoke.

"Not the first time you runned away, I bet. Eh?

Blaise nods.

He crawls to the door and lifts the flap. "We gots company."
Blaise crawls over and looks out just in time to see two policemen pluck the 109 from its hiding place.

"Hey Sarge, look here." Cops cluster. One with stripes on his jacket comes down from the cruiser. He turns the boat in gloved fingers, pops it in a plastic sack, and sits it like a criminal thing in the car's back seat. Blaise thinks how safe it would feel to be caged in there and have the adventure over with.

"Don't think, kid," says Inkman. "Yer better with me than in the Parkdale cop shop. That place is full o' stories. But we got to move. They'll pulp us if they find us. I know a crawl place they couldn't dream of. Let's make for the Source."

They wiggle under the brush. Last year's acorns fill his pockets. Burrs clot his sweater while Inkman's feet work in the mud inches from his nose, PF Flyers with high-tops that flap, laceless, at the ankles.

"It's the rotary movement you look for," Inkman mumbles. "Holy coagulation. Glut on the salt of its wisdom!"

The bare branches make Blaise feel like he's looking up at the tattered sky from inside a cage of bones. His insignia hangs by a single pin. A sculpture garden rears up behind a scribble of dogwood, imaginings made from logs and steel and cables.

"Rot your socks, kid," Inkman wheezes. "We're almost here!"

They scramble down a bank where black roots make a staircase and cross the road into a stand of willows. There's nobody. They've beaten the cops to it.

"We're on the final ground so step in the shit. Puts them off your scent. Ha!"

Around one of the willows there's a carved wooden snake with feathers for scales, painted green, bloody-lipped and fangy. Beyond the snake there's a pond with islands and bridges and a concrete temple thing. But the water is pure filth, pea green, and scummed with cloudy glops. He and Inkman slink under the willows.

"Keep your eye on the sky," says the Inkman. "The minute you get near the Source, the whirling bird appears."

And it does: a heron, blue and beaky and huge, settles on the opposite shore. A dead fountain spews nothing in the pond's middle. At the top end, the ground rises in a steep bank, Bloor Street booming at the top.

In the middle of the bank a culvert hole drizzles slop into the pond.

"There it is, kid. That's what yer lookin' fer. The Source."

The only way to get to the culvert is through the water. Inkman wades in up to his knees and hoists himself into the Source's mouth. "C'mon, we've made it. Here's your chance."

You can hear the squawk of police radios back in the willows.

"Time's up," says Inkman, jiggling like someone who needs to pee. "They catch us and we're fertilizer."

Blaise jumps in the water. Ooze grabs his ankles like the fingers of dead Grenadiers. He squelches toward the culvert.

"This is it kid," Inkman says as he backs into the sulphur-smelling darkness. "This is where it all begins. C'mon."

Back on shore, the policemen call his name. Blaise turns and sees that his father is with them, wrapped in a car coat and wearing his fur hat. He plucks off his National Rescue Patrol insignia, turns it white side out, and sticks it on the end of his Johnny Seven. He hoists his flag high and offers his surrender.

The Pot

"You think I am crazy when I tell you a pot is an angel of God."
Pani Magda Zielinska had taken over as babysitter and den mother to the street when Borzena Sigalski died, a year or so after Blaise started school. She had two little boys of her own and looked after three others plus Blaise and me, who still came for lunch from time to time as we got older, when our mother was having one of her episodes. Blaise was still young enough to watch cartoons with the little ones until it was time to walk back to St. Bridget's School with us. But Therese and I weren't interested in cartoons anymore, so we sat at the kitchen table while Magda told her stories and teased us. I thought she was going to tease us now, as she reached over with an arm that looked as though it had been boiled with beetroots and set the pot down in the middle of the table.

It was a metal saucepan, dented all around its lip with spots of rust where the handle had been reattached.

"It's not much to look at," Magda said, "but look and I tell you how the little things save lives. One afternoon during the war, I sat with my mother while she fed my little brother Jacek his *kasha* from this same pot in our front garden ..."

So it was going to be a story. Stories were better than teasing. Lately Magda had been teasing me about girls and teasing Therese about boys and teasing both of us about each other. She had been telling Therese about the things she should be putting under her pillow and how she should make a wreath and set it adrift on the Humber River so that it could be found by her true love. And then she'd look at me and wink.

"Our town was a garrison and, always, the ground was shaking with German trucks passing our house. I wasn't afraid of Germans. The soldiers were always coming to our fence, saying how Jacek and I reminded them of their own kids and showing us pictures. These weren't like the men who shot your uncles, Aleksei. These Germans gave us chocolate or little toys they had made from the wood of bombed-out buildings. At the same time, my mother did laundry for the partisans in the forests. When the soldiers noticed how much men's clothing hung on our line, they warned her that their colonel would shoot her, *piff-paff*, like that, if he ever noticed. They could have been shot themselves, just for warning us.

"The planes were always coming and going over our heads, so often that we had gotten lazy about taking cover. On the afternoon I'm thinking of, the sky filled with airplanes until my teeth started to hum with the noise of them. My mother kept feeding Jacek from this same pot you see in front of you, while my father and grandfather made a sport of guessing, from the sound of the engines, whose planes they were.

"'Russian,' my father said.

"'No, German,' my grandfather insisted.

"When the bombs started to whistle over our heads, my father shouted, 'Ha! I told you. Russians!'"

It's amazing that I remember Magda's story at all. Because, at the time, all I could think about was Therese, though it wasn't exactly thinking, more just an awareness of her across the table from me, the light from the kitchen window setting off bright crescents in her braids, the tawny colour of her forearms, the paleness of her blue eyes. We had always called her Terenia, but she insisted on being called Therese after we started taking French in grade seven. We had grown up together on Galway Avenue. There were pictures of us in my mother's album, side by side on the kiddie swings at High Park. But now I was seeing someone different whenever she was in a room with me, and sensing a kind of guilty secret that I couldn't quite put together.

"The pilots were always aiming for the rail yards on the far side of town. But that day the Russians were off target. The first bomb hit the house two doors over from us. I remember an orange flash and a smack of wind. Then everything went black with flying dirt, and Jacek began to cry and the animals tied up in our neighbours' yards began to scream and we were running. With one hand I held tight to my mother. In the other I carried this pot, still full of Jacek's *kasha*.

"I had it in my head that, as long I didn't spill any of it, God would be good to us. So I didn't spill a single grain, not even when we dived for cover under a big truck in the middle of the road. I hugged the pot close even when some soldiers pulled us back into the road shouting. *Nein! Nein, matka! Benzine! Benzine!*

"It was a petrol lorry, you see. If a bomb had hit, we would have been *frytki*. So then we were running with the soldiers to the barracks at the end of the road. '*Matka! Matka! Kommen sie!*' they shouted and waved us toward the cellar door and their bomb shelter. But there was no room. The soldiers pushed and pushed to get us in so that I had a hard time to keep from dumping *kasha* all down the front of me. They couldn't get the doors closed and we were forced back into the road.

"So we ran again. My hand was like iron around that handle you see in front of you. I don't think my mother knew where we were running really, just away, away from the smell of burning animals and gasoline, from splinters that whizzed past our ears. I remember passing a stable that had just been hit and the air was full of little tongues of burning hay that made me think of the Pentecost. But you couldn't think of anything for more than a second what with all the screaming. It was worst as we ran past the wall of the place where they kept Jews, out in the open, with nothing to protect them during the air raids."

Therese got up from the table and began clearing the plates. I watched her hands with the long piano fingers that made her so much better at playing Chopin than I would ever be. She went to the sink, set the dishes in the water and began wiping them clean, her weight on one leg, the other bent like a stork's. She came back to the table and I noticed the warm, soapy smell of her as she gathered up the knives and forks, leaving nothing between Magda and me except her beaten-up old pot.

"I kept a hold on this pot and God didn't disappoint me. The fires and the explosions fell behind us as we reached the outskirts of town. We carried the smell of burning on our clothes right into the house of my mother's cousin, a beekeeper who lived at the edge of the forest.

"The beekeeper's wife had to pry the handle out of my fingers and I cried and cried as they scooped the *kasha*, which was full of cinders by now, into the garbage. So they washed the pot up and gave it back to me. That night, and for every night during the rest of the war, I slept with it. Every time we heard an airplane, Jacek would cry

'Mama, mama, the bombs are falling on me!' and I would put the pot on my head.

"My father dug a bomb shelter in our back garden after that. I remember his silhouette in the doorway against nights lit up like a summer day. I remember feeling certain that the pilots could see me crouching there and feeling just as sure that I was safe as long as I wore this pot, my little *kasketka*, on my head."

Magda reached across the table and gave me a playful swat with the tea towel she had been wearing over her shoulder.

"Are you on the moon, Aleksei?" she asked.

I should have been listening. Stories like Magda's were all around us, but they were things the grownups whispered after the children went to bed. By telling us this story of the pot, I realized she was trying to confer something on us, but I couldn't have said what that something was, any more than I could have defined the feelings rustling around inside me as Therese snatched the pot off the table, dunked it in the sink and worked at it with a scouring pad until it seemed it would never be clean.

Constitution Day

Poniatowski bent smartly from the waist, clicked his heels, and planted a kiss between the woman's swollen knuckles.

"Oh Pan Poniatowski, the pleasure is mine. An honour to be of service. Don't you look dashing this evening?"

He caught a glimpse of himself in the mirror under the staircase. His diet of exile had kept him a little too slim and the sable lapels of his overcoat sagged where his chest should have been, but the flashes of white that the dye had left at his temples under the brim of his grey homburg did indeed add a touch of drama to his appearance.

"Truly, Pani Cybulka, I am grateful. My humble accommodations are not suitable for such business."

"Yes, I'm sorry that we can't offer you permanent rooms here. But we must charge what the market will bear."

"I meant only that I suspect my lodgings are under surveillance."

"The consulate?"

"Quite possibly. I have twice seen cars with diplomatic plates parked in front of my rooming house. The situation is very unstable. This business in Prague."

"Do you think the Czechs will succeed?"

"Our prayers are with them, Pani Cybulka. This could be the beginning of what we have been waiting for. I could be called away to London at any moment. I must ensure that our business here is in capable hands."

This was loose talk and he knew it. He was being boastful, indiscreet.

"Not Pan Skrubicki, I hope. He's here. I've already taken another bottle up to him."

"No, Pani Cybulka. Up till now, I haven't had the luxury of picking and choosing our activists, but that is about to change. Tonight I have invited Pan Mienkiewicz to join us."

Another indiscretion, but surely one worth making to lift the spirits of his most devoted and unquestioning supporter.

"Pan Mienkiewicz? Truly? Such a fine man! A saint. Only last night my cousin's widow was telling me about all that he has done for her. Took care of everything after the accident, the lawyers, the accountants, the police. He'll be a great help to our cause."

She led him up the oak stairs and down a dim hallway that smelled of unwashed bachelors to the sun room tacked on to the back of the house.

"One of your guests is already here," she said as they reached the closed door at the end of the hall. "My son Romek is home to answer the door for Pan Mienkiewicz and the others and to bring you whatever you need. I will go out shortly to evening mass — for Constitution Day."

"Of course."

The sunroom was furnished with mismatched furniture whose

split seams were disguised with swatches of embroidered linen. The blinds had been drawn on all the windows and the room was lit by two aging floor lamps and a pair of candlesticks on the table Pani Cybulka had set with bottles of vodka and plum brandy, glasses of cut crystal, plates of sausage and pickles, and a dish of herring with sour cream. Poniatowski's old nemesis, Pavel Skrubicki, stood over the spread like a crow ready to strike.

"Our hostess has provided well for us," Poniatowski observed as he set down his battered attaché case.

Skrubicki worked his fingers over the food and sniffed disdainfully.

"I confess that lately my tastes have shifted to caviar."

"Still affecting Russian airs, Pan Skrubicki?"

"Not at all. Caviar is Baltic. The Swedes eat it. So do the Finns. Why not us? Brandy?"

He poured two shots, downed one, and then the other after Poniatowski waved it away.

"*Na zdrowie.*"

"You should be drinking to the Constitution."

"I will; when I find a compatriot willing to share a toast with me."

"*Touché,*" said Poniatowski. He should have been better at masking his contempt. This was a new kind of war, and men like Skrubicki had their uses.

"While we're waiting for the others why don't you update me on our recruiting drive?"

"Eh — well — of the list you gave me, let's see." Skrubicki extracted a creased, heavily pencilled sheet of paper from his pocket and put on his reading glasses, one of the arms of which was secured with a twist of copper wire. So far we've signed up thirty-two new members."

"That's not enough. We need at least a hundred more to guarantee our man the nomination."

Skrubicki tossed a stack of blank membership cards onto a side table. "I can't just give these things away. Sadly there are rules and they have to be paid for. Now if we had some cash to spread around ..."

"Fundraising is a matter I hope to take up with Pan Mienkiewicz."

"He really is coming, eh?"

"You don't seem pleased."

"Our history is complicated you know."

"You owe the Trust money?"

"You know, Pan Poniatowski. You really must try one of these *ogórki*." Skrubicki munched on the snub end of a pickle. "They are exquisite. I don't know what Pani Cybulka does with her brine but the effect is magical."

A volley of laughter rumbled at the foot of the stairs, followed by heavy steps on the landing.

"Where are they hiding themselves? The old plotters."

"They're in here, Pan Duchacek." Pani Cybulka's son Romek opened the door to reveal Tom Duchacek lighting the hall with his new false teeth.

"Aha! So there you are, Poniatowski old boy. Standing at attention like you expect General Piłsudski himself to walk through this door."

More laughter, with Skrubicki joining in.

"Have a drink, Tomek."

Duchacek accepted a glass, clinked with Skrubicki, then set it down on the sideboard without drinking. He surveyed Poniatowski from head to toe.

"And what, Ignacy? You going to take off your coat and hat? You look dressed for Siberia in that getup."

Poniatowski waited till the two men had turned their attention to the food before slipping out of his coat, folding it over the back of a chair and setting his homburg carefully atop it.

"That's better," Duchacek said through a mouthful of sausage. "Now the suit, I hear that pinstripes are coming back, but only for hippies. I tell you what. If we win, I'll take you down to Jack Fraser's and buy you some proper casual clothes."

He struck a pose, offering his lemon-yellow sweater, check trousers, and white loafers as a model. Poniatowski swallowed on his disgust. Duchacek didn't care a fig that Poniatowski's suit was cut in Saville Row, that it had been worn at palaces and embassies, and in the offices of generals and prime ministers. He was a true vulgarian and, like Skrubicki, infuriatingly vital to his cause.

"You are looking well, Pan Duchacek. I trust your business is thriving."

"It's a good time to be in demolition, Pan Poniatowski. This city can't wait to get rid of itself. They're knocking down building after building. And we're expanding into waste disposal. The future is in garbage."

Duchacek paused long enough to allow Skrubicki to mumble in agreement.

"Where is the man of the hour? Mienkiewicz. He's coming isn't he?"

"He'll come," said Poniatowski. "He's an officer, a cavalryman, a man of his word."

"Cavalry? I thought Mienkiewicz was air force."

"Both. He was in the cavalry in '39." Skrubicki interjected. "Joined the air force in England."

"I saw his regiment on parade in '38," Poniatowski added, aware that he and Skrubicki are now vying for Duchacek's attention. "Magnificent. The picture of gallantry."

"And meanwhile the Germans were coming in tanks. So much for your gallantry."

"It's what got us through."

"It's what got some of you through, old boy, you lot in London. The rest of us — who were left at home — we got through on our wits."

"Gentlemen, I think it's time for a toast," said Skrubicki. "You won't deny me now, Poniatowski, not with Pan Duchacek here. To the Constitution of 1791!"

Poniatowski lifted his glass. "And to Poland in her borders of 1939."

"You can't be serious."

"It is our birthright."

"What will you do with all those people who've been resettled? Put them on the moon?"

"I have presented a detailed plan of repatriation to the government-in-exile."

"You? A detailed plan? To that gang of quarrelsome tobacconists? Even the Vatican doesn't recognize them anymore."

Poniatowski downed his vodka at a shot. "If you'll excuse me, gentlemen. I will call to our guest, to see what has delayed him."

"Send up the boy," Skrubicki called after him.

DUCHACEK WATCHED THE DIPLOMAT make his exit, sighed, then tested the springs of the armchair to see if it would support him.

"And so, Skrubicki, how's your business? Staying away from the ponies I hope. Last I heard, you were going to lose some fingers if you showed your face at Greenwood again."

"My business is entirely legitimate. I have a full house, now they've closed the Lakeview Psychiatric Hospital."

"So you are master of your own personal lunatic asylum."

"Of two asylums, Pan Duchacek. Outpatients are the best tenants. They never ask if their accommodation meets the standard and their rent comes straight from the government."

"So you are a client of the state. You should be supporting Trudeau and his socialists."

A soft knock sounded at the door and Romek slipped into the room wearing the khaki uniform of the Polish scouts.

"Pan Poniatowski said you were asking for me."

"Ah, Romek. We will be needing another bottle before we're through."

"That's all that was ordered. There's only the bottle my father keeps in the garage."

"Bring that. Tell him the Progressive Conservative Party will pay."

"*Tak jest.*" The boy saluted and disappeared down the hall.

Skrubicki took a blank membership card from the stack, held it to one of the candlesticks and lit a cigarette.

"Trudeau's man," he explained, "our Member of Parliament, the doctor, has not been a great supporter of my endeavours. Wants the hospitals reopened. The other party is, I think, more sympathetic to the entrepreneur."

"You think they stand a chance?"

"They do if we can get our man the nomination, one of our own — and if we can get Mienkiewicz to support him for the nomination — well — people would vote for a donkey if they knew Mienkiewicz was for him."

"Too bad we don't have a donkey."

"You don't care for our man Lukashchenko, Pan Duchacek?"

"He's Ukrainian."

"Better than some retired Scotsman. Poniatowski likes him."

"Poniatowski likes him because, like Poniatowski, Lukashchenko sees communists under every carpet. Some people still go for that kind of thing, but Prague is just the beginning and most people around here have heard that Stalin is dead. And a Ukrainian, well, you never know with them, do you? Have you checked his war record?"

"Mienkiewicz doesn't mind Ukrainians. It was Ukrainians who got him out of Poland."

"Yes, it all comes down to Mienkiewicz. Pan Tadeusz. Guys like him scare me. They refuse to play the game. Tried to score a loan off him last year, a little venture capital. He knows who my friends are, what I could do for him. But the bastard told me to go up the street to the Dominion Bank. He wants to give it all to orphans and bricklayers."

"So then why are you here, Pan Duchacek?"

"Same reason as you, Pan Skrubicki. We're both gambling men. We want to back a winner. And, in the unlikely event that Mienkiewicz backs your Lukashchenko, we just might have one."

"I'll drink to that!" Skrubicki drained the last of the plum brandy. "Where's our fearless leader gone, I wonder?"

"I suspect he's calling on different spirits from yours, old boy."

"The spirit of Kościuszko!"

"Of Sikorski!"

"Of Paderewski."

They laughed.

"We shouldn't laugh."

"No."

"I'm surprised Poniatowski doesn't have a go at the nomination himself."

"Can't. He's not a citizen. Refuses to take the oath to the Queen. 'I will not be made a British object,' he says. Ah, but look who's come to cheer us up. R-r-r-r-omek."

The boy entered the room, the bottle clasped like the sacrament in two hands. "I'm sorry it took so long, sirs. The bottle wasn't in the usual place, I had to hunt for it."

"That's what boy scouts do. Scout for things, no?"

"That's right, sir."

"Still wearing your uniform, I see."

"Yes. In honour of the Constitution."

"'The last will and testament of the expiring Motherland!'"

"The second constitution in the world. The first in all of Europe."

"The boy knows his history. Did you march in the parade this morning?"

"I did, sir. From High Park all the way to St. Voytek's."

"That must have tired you out!"

"Not a bit, Pan Duchacek. I'd like to be a soldier and fight for Poland like my father and all his friends."

"Well then, you'll have to learn to drink like a soldier. You want to try? Here." Skrubicki filled the shot glass and handed it to the boy, who held it at arm's length, expecting it to explode. "Go on, boy. Don't try to sip it. Knock it back in one go. It'll make a soldier of you."

The boy complied. The line of his mouth pulled tight against the searing in his throat.

"Taken like a true soldier. Now can you sing? Polish soldiers love to sing."

Skrubicki opened his mouth and sang in a moist, tuneless voice. "*March, march, Polonia. March brave nation ...*"

"Um, I don't really sing, sir. But I can recite."

"Well then, let's hear it."

PONIATOWSKI STOOD ON THE Cybulka's porch for as long as the thinning material of his suit would allow in the chilled evening air of early spring. He had exhausted all his avenues, called first to the Mienkiewicz home where one of his boys said his father was out on business, couldn't say where or when he was expected, then to the Parish Trust, forgetting it was a Sunday and finding no answer, then to the Combatant's Association where there was a dinner for Constitution Day. Mienkiewicz, the porter's voice said, had come and gone. He tried Zaleski, Tymbach — no answer, no luck. Then a second call to Mienkiewicz, this time reaching his wife, Marlene.

"Pani Mienkiewicz, if you please, I am looking for your husband."

"Well, Mr. Poniatowski, aren't we all?"

The voice at the other end of the line sounded harsh and, at the same time, fragile, about to snap.

"We have been expecting him at a meeting. A very important meeting. And he is now an hour late."

"My husband is expected at a lot of meetings, Mr. Poniatowski, and they're all important. I'm sure he'll turn up there long before he turns up here. And when he does, could you remind him that he has a home and a family?"

Another fifteen minutes, a half hour, he had no idea how long he stood breathing in the hints of magnolia and apple blossom in the boulevard that swept down to the park gates. There was nothing more to do, no further avenues to pursue, and so he trudged back up the stairs, rehearsing the excuses he would make to the others. He stopped at the door when he heard the boy's thin voice breaking into verse:

> Hail, O Christ, Thou Lord of Men!
> Poland in Thy footsteps treading
> Like Thee suffers, at Thy bidding;
> Like Thee, too, shall rise again.

Poniatowski opened the door to the back room just as Skrubicki was administering another shot of vodka. He moved to take it from the boy, when Duchacek interrupted him with a tap on his watch glass.

"And so, Poniatowski old boy, it looks like, once again, your cavalry fails to arrive."

First Flight

The bus, one of the type left over from the war that regular air force personnel called a "Green Monster," stopped and spit them out beside the parade square. Leading Air Cadet Margate, Leading Air Cadet Skrebensky, and Leading Air Cadet Mienkiewicz had special orders. They had been chosen by the squadron commander to attend the Senior NCO Course at this year's summer camp. If they passed the course, they would become bona fide senior non-commissioned officers, jump the rank of corporal, and go straight to sergeant.

"This squadron has some things to live down after Bagotville," Captain Orlowski had wheezed through the stem of his pipe before they left the city. "We're counting on you three to put things right."

The bus discharged them into a group of thirty-odd cadets who milled about in the shade of one of the large maples that lined the square. Alex checked the squadron ID on their shoulder flashes: 241 Oshawa, 302 Windsor, 516 Smith Falls, 95 Sudbury. The largest contingent was from 701 Ottawa squadron, most of them with corporal stripes already on their sleeves. They stood apart from everyone else, smoking, adjusting the knots of their ties, dusting their toecaps in case of a surprise inspection. They spoke only to each other until one, a tall blond corporal, spied Skrebensky and said, "Hey guys, if it ain't the One-Nine-Three from the big Tee-Oh. The heroes of Faggotville have returned."

When an Officer Cadet in summer dress marched out of the heat snakes rising off the square and shouted the order, Alex, Margate, and Skrebensky made a point of being the first to fall in. Margate, the longest of leg, was first to get to the prized right marker's position two paces in front of the OC. Alex drew up on his left and dressed his position, right arm raised straight and true so that the knuckle just grazed Newgate's shoulder flash. Skrebensky lined up on Alex so that the rest of the flight would have to dress positions on them, the cadets from 193 Queen City Squadron.

"Wo-o-o-o, the LACs from Faggotville are keeners," someone muttered as the ranks filled in behind them.

Alex didn't look left or right, refused to notice the ribbing any more than he acknowledged the heat pressing through his wool battle dress. He gave all his concentration to his position of attention, as per the *Canadian Forces Manual of Drill and Ceremonial*:

a. heels together and in line;
b. feet turned out to form an angle of 30 degrees;
c. body balanced and weight distributed evenly on both feet;
d. shoulders level, square to the front;
e. arms hanging as straight as their natural bend will allow, with elbows and wrists touching the body;

f. wrists straight, the back of the hands outwards;

g. fingers aligned, touching the palm of the hand, thumbs placed
    on the side of the forefinger at the middle joint with the thumbs
    and back of the fingers touching the thighs lightly and the
    thumbs in line with the seam of the trousers; and

h. head held erect, neck touching the back of the collar, eyes
    steady, looking their height and straight to the front.

He was in formation with his wingmates, Skrebensky and Margate.
Together, they were unflinchable.

"HEY MCKNIGHT."

"What is it, Horner?"

"They gonna let us fly, you think?"

"Check the schedule, dickweed. It's on the board."

Horner was number one sidekick to McKnight, the blond Ottawa
corporal. He skulked over to the corkboard hung on the side of the
communal locker in which the flight's trench coats and battledress
were stowed. The rest of the wing were playing pool and Ping-Pong
at the canteen, or at a screening of *The Great Escape* at the amphi-
theatre, but the Senior NCO Course was restricted to quarters, shining
their shoes, polishing brass, taking turns at the ironing board where
they struggled to press their newly issued summer dress (khaki shorts
and shirts, knee socks with red-ribboned garters) into the required
seams and angles.

"Oh, yeah. Says right here. 'Transport flight.' This Thursday afternoon. Then we got gliding next Wednesday."

"What do you think they'll send us up in?"

"Dunno. They got Herculeses here. And 707s, the ones they fly
Trudeau around in."

"Ah, they'll prob'ly send us up in one of those old DC-3s. We gotta be the last air force in the world flying those things."

"If they do, don't eat beans before you go up. Those planes aren't pressurized. They take you high enough and you fart your brains out."

McKnight lay on his top bunk and turned the pages of a water-skiing magazine. His shoes were already shined, his brass was already gleaming, but there was no sign of shoe polish on his fingers, no rag with chalky stains of Brasso in his kit. Things happened for McKnight as if by magic. He'd been last man into the tent that afternoon, but still ended up with the top bunk furthest from the drafty flaps. And sometimes the magic wasn't so magical: at mess parade, he took the right marker's spot after Horner and the other Ottawa cadets had shouldered Margate out of the way.

"Next time we're at Faggotville, I'm going up in a CF-5," McKnight announced.

"Fuck off."

"Nobody goes up in a fighter."

"I will."

"McKnight here is air force royalty," Horner explained to no one in particular.

"Oh yeah?" Margate looked up with sudden interest from the brass buttons of his wedge cap.

"Well," sighed McKnight, "if you must know …," and in bored singsong he told the tent about his uncle: Squadron Leader Willie McKnight, World War II ace with twenty victories in a Spitfire during the Battle of France and the Battle of Britain. Killed in action over the channel in 1941.

"Err — hmmm."

Skrebensky got up from his bunk and stood in the at-ease position — feet exactly six inches apart, hands folded behind his back, thumbs locked, fingers pointing flat and straight — a stance he tended to adopt whenever he was a little nervous (which was most of the time).

"I think you have some of your facts wrong, Corporal McKnight."

"Oh really?"

"Yes — errmm — Willie McKnight had eighteen kills, not twenty. And he got them in a Hurricane. Canadian squadrons didn't get Spits until almost 1942. He was never a squadron leader, either. McKnight was still just a Pilot Officer when he died."

Stony silence among the Ottawa cadets. McKnight stared down at Skrebensky, over the edge of a full-page portrait of water-ski champ George Athens, and smiled his pointy smile. Skreb did his best to return the smile, but his face buckled in one of the intense, eye-scrunching blinks that were a habit of his and Alex saw what McKnight was seeing, a flossy-haired child-man with a spastic face. The hair on his cropped neck bristled. He should have been swooping to his wingmate's defence, covering his tail. But they were outgunned and outranked. Margate stayed out of the fray, his deep brown features set on the flecks of dried Brasso he was removing from his cap badge with a toothbrush. In the end, Skrebensky was spared by the appearance of an even more vulnerable target for McKnight's wolf pack.

"Wow! Elliot!"

LAC Wilf Elliot of 116 Chatham Squadron had just removed his T-shirt, revealing an angry purple field of acne blemishes to the tent.

"Wha—?" Elliot wheeled to confront his attackers with small features set too close together on the large pale disk of his face.

"What you got on your back there?"

He cast a glance over his right shoulder and made a face.

"Just zits."

"Ah."

McKnight assessed his new target, glanced back at George Athens as if he were looking for a point of comparison.

"Hey, Elliot."

"Yah?"

"You got your masturbation papers?"

RAIN BLEW IN OFF Lake Ontario before dawn and, by reveille, it was beating quick time on their canvas ceiling. The Senior NCO course moaned out of their bunks after a night of sleep made fitful by Elliot's snores. McKnight, the first one dressed, moved to the tent door and raised the flap.

"Gentlemen, get your trench coats out. We are truly fucked."

The campground was awash in shoeshine-obliterating ooze and Officer Cadet Burns chose the deepest spot for fall-in. Alex listed into the muck like a scuttled flying boat as the OC called roll and the ground sucked at the soles of his Oxfords. When Burns called the order to march, Elliot lost a shoe and had to dig for it, filthying his hands and the tails of his coat. The rain became a barrage of steel needles and it dyed their sky-blue trench coats a deep navy as they marched the mile-long trek to the parade square. The road was as pocked as Passchendaele and the OC steered the flight through the deepest craters, sending mucky water up shins and calves. By the time they reached the square, ankle socks slouched like punctured barrage balloons and garter ribbons trailed in the mud.

The flight wheeled twice around the tarmac then halted opposite the enlisted men's mess, where they stood at attention for an eternity, stomachs turning barrel rolls at the smell of frying fat. The regular squadron flights straggled onto the square in ragged columns and fell out immediately to the mess. Morning inspection had been cancelled for everyone except the Senior NCO course.

Finally, Lieutenant Andersson emerged from the officers' mess and shot toward them at a quick march. The course commander still wore the blue of the pre-unification air force. The albatross on his cap badge gleamed through raindrops that refused to land on the aerodynamic folds of his coat.

"Well ladies," he called as soon as he was within earshot, "even from here I can tell that you've all just failed your first inspection."

OC Burns came to attention with a crack of his cleated shoe. Salutes were exchanged and Andersson began his progress along the ranks, clucking at every gaffe in the cadets' rain-tormented dress. Some drew fire for their fogged brass, others took hits for the muddy paste on their shoes. Elliot got flak from head to toe for his muck-spattered appearance. By the time Andersson got to Skrebensky, nervous tics were running riot all over the cadet's face, tongue darting uncontrollably from the corner of his mouth.

"LAC, what is that, er, thing protruding from your face?"

"M-m-m-my tongue, sir."

"Well, keep it where it belongs. We don't want you infecting everyone else."

Coming to Margate, the Lieutenant took a step back and stared him straight in the eye.

"You are?"

"Margate, sir!"

"My, you certainly are black, aren't you?"

"Yes, sir!"

"Is that going to be a problem?"

"No, sir!"

"Good."

McKnight was the only cadet in the flight Andersson already knew by name.

"And you must be McKnight."

"Yes, sir!"

The Lieutenant sized him up, nodded, and moved on without comment.

Alex forgot all about his sodden appearance when Andersson came abreast of him. He felt transfixed in the sights of a serving officer with pilots wings over his breast pocket, a man who might soon be piercing the edge of space in a Starfighter.

"What's your name, LAC?"

"Mienkiewicz, *sir!*"

"Well, LAC Menkywitz, it's time to get rid of that peach fuzz. Buy a razor."

It was as if he'd been awarded the Victoria Cross.

Andersson completed his sweep and returned to the front rank, stood himself at ease while the flight remained at attention.

"In light of this morning's dismal showing, I am cancelling today's scheduled tour of the hangars. Camp offers many frivolous delights to the average cadet. But you are not average cadets, are you ...," Andersson consulted the roster on OC Burns's clipboard, "... Elliot?"

"Nun-no sir."

"What are you, Elliot?"

"Above average cadets, sir?"

"Wrong, Elliot. For your penance you will get down on all fours where you belong and give me twenty-five."

Elliot fell out to a spot indicated by OC Burns, where water had pooled on the asphalt. He grunted to his knees and began a series of flaccid push-ups as Andersson continued his oration. "Cadets," he said, "welcome to the worst two weeks of your pathetic young lives. But at the end of it, you'll have learned a very important thing about yourselves. You will have learned which of the two great categories of humanity you fall into: leaders or followers. For reasons that escape me, your squadrons have an inkling you fall into the former category.

For me, it will be most amusing to try and figure out what your COS could have been thinking.

"I'll tell you what you are, gentlemen. You are maggots — not worthy of the muck from whence you have wriggled. No progress is possible without your accepting this. What are you, gentlemen?"

"Maggots, sir!"

"And so we make a beginning."

Andersson turned on his heel and marched back to the officer's mess, leaving Elliot struggling at his push-ups.

ARCHERY, CANCELLED. SAILING, CANCELLED. Rifle range, cancelled. The Senior NCO course was confined to barracks pending improvement of its dress and deportment.

"Look at these shoes," hissed Margate. "Shit. One parade and a whole year's worth of shine is gone."

"Shouldn't be a problem for you, Margate," said Horner. "Shoe-shining is in the genes with you people, isn't it?"

Guffaws all around from the Ottawa crowd. Margate pretended not to hear and concentrated on the dried mud in the creases in his shoes.

"Gentlemen, gentlemen," McKnight intervened. "There is no place for racism in this man's air force. Say Margate, where'd you learn to iron like that?"

McKnight points to Margate's summer dress, pressed into razor sharp creases on a hanger over his bunk.

Margate shrugged. "When you come from Regent Park, you learn to look after yourself."

"I'll make you a deal. I help you with those shoes, you help me with my uniform."

"Deal."

"Right, let me introduce you to the fine art of burning in a shine."
The Ottawa gang admitted Margate to their circle at McKnight's
feet as he caked shoe polish on the toe of his water-fogged Oxford,
then plucked the match he'd been chewing on from between his
teeth. He struck it on the bottom rail of his bed and held the shoe
over the flame with a quick roll of the wrist. Then he tossed away
the spent match and took up a soft cloth, stretched it over his fore-
finger, and worked the melted polish into the leather in tiny circles.

"Just like a spit polish. 'Cept the shit in your saliva doesn't cloud
up the shine. Trick is not to hold any one spot of your shoe over the
flame too long. Otherwise you burn the leather and you're fucked."

Margate drew himself onto McKnight's bunk and repeated the
steps with his own shoes and, soon enough, the two cadets possessed
shoes that shone like polished onyx.

"Thanks, McKnight."

"No need to thank me, Margate." McKnight tossed an armload
of wrinkled khakis into Margate's face. "We got a deal, remember?"

While the rest of the flight watched the demonstration, Skrebensky
slipped out of the tent carrying the shoes he'd been spit polishing.
Alex found him on a bench at the basketball court near the fence
where the Trans-Canada Highway bisected the base.

"Hey Skreb, what you doing?"

He held up a flesh-coloured wad of material.

"My secret weapon."

It was a woman's nylon stocking.

"McKnight is full of shit. Best way is still a spit polish, but you've
got to use one of these to finish it off."

He took the stocking and bunched it in his fingers to make a pad
and worked it lightly over the leather.

"See? Takes off the dirt and the caked-on polish, leaves a nice hard
finish."

"Nice!"

"I've got a spare one. I'll make you a deal."

"Sure."

"I'll give it to you ...," Skrebensky grinned and flicked his tongue, "... if you put it on for me first."

"HEY ELLIOT," SAID MCKNIGHT in the dark after lights out.

"What?"

"You're a farm boy right?"

"Yeah."

"Is it true what they say about farmers and their pigs?"

"Huh?"

"Well, it's just I knew this farm girl from Arnprior. Her sister had a boyfriend did time in prison. After he got out, the guy admitted he'd been involved in ho-mo-sexual activity while he was inside. 'How did it make you feel?' she asked. 'Well,' her sister answered. 'it was like that time we saw Daddy with the pig.' That how things work down around Chatham, Smelliot?"

"No, it isn't"

"You smell like you've been up close with some pigs. We been here four days and you haven't had a shower."

"Pigs are very clean animals if you want to know, and I fuckin' wash."

"But you don't fuckin' shower."

"No way I'm goin' in that shower tent. I heard what happens in there."

"Oh yeah? And what have you heard."

"Someone gets a boner, by accident, like, and they — you know, like that guy at Bagotville."

"Ah, well, that's something our boys from the One-Nine-Three could tell us about. LAC Blinky, why don't you enlighten us."

"Shut up, McKnight. My name's Skrebensky."

"I heard they shaved a guy's dick off," said Horner.

"Yeah then they covered his crotch in shoe polish," added another Ottawa cadet.

"I heard it was Deep Heat. Fuckin' fried his nuts off. Guy ended up in hospital," added a third.

"The thing is, Smelliot," said McKnight, "that kind of stuff doesn't have to happen in the shower. It could happen anywhere. It could happen right here, in this tent. Unless, of course, you already have your masturbation papers."

Someone snickered into his pillow. Elliot contemplated the scorched finish on his shoes then looked up at McKnight.

"So how do I get these papers?"

"There's two ways. First there's the Faggotville way, which is the hard way. Then there's the easy way. All you do is march up to Lieutenant Andersson and ask for them. It's like a ritual. All the officers know about it."

LIEUTENANT ANDERSSON STOOD BY the classroom window and stared down at the parade square where Elliot ran double time round the periphery, a drill rifle held over his head, as punishment for that morning's insubordination. Even after the lieutenant had torn a strip off him for the state of his shoes, he had mustered the courage to request his masturbation papers in front of the whole flight. Suspecting that others had put Elliot up to it, he announced that he was cancelling their transport flight. Indefinitely.

"You may laugh at Mr. Elliot, gentlemen. But he's taking his punishment. No whining. No complaining. That's an important test of leadership. If you can't take the punishment, how can you expect your subordinates to? That was the secret of our success at Ypres, Vimy, Falaise, Ortona. We won those battles because the mines, the lumber camps, and the fisheries and our godforsaken winters taught us how to take a beating. Punishment. Failure. That's what brings you face to face with who you really are."

McKnight and his cronies (who now included Margate) exchanged obscene notes and sketches when the co wasn't looking, but Alex paid rapt attention. Andersson is Cliff Robertson in 633 *Squadron*, Gregory Peck in *Twelve O'Clock High* and Robert Shaw in *The Battle of Britain* all rolled into one. Alex wants him to see that he's ready to fail, ready for whatever punishment the officer sees fit to bestow on him.

"It's a confused world out there, gentlemen. Hippies, yippies, separatists, hijackers, drug dealers, and everyone thinking they can just do their own thing. That's not our world, gentlemen. We're the ones who have to keep our heads. We're the ones they'll count on when the party's over. We have to see things the way they really are. Because this world is an unforgiving world. Anybody remember the Starfighter that crashed at Cold Lake last year? The pilot went straight in at six hundred miles an hour. Know why? He took three seconds to check his radio settings while climbing through overcast. That's how forgiving life in the air is. I'm not going to be any more forgiving with you."

The building vibrated in a long descending bass note and a huge shadow slipped across the windows. A Hercules, or maybe an Argus or an Aurora coming in to refuel on its way back to Shearwater. The cadets had to check their desire to run to the window for a look. The regular squadrons had been going up for circuits of the field in a noisy old Otter. But, for the Senior NCO course, there was only drill, drill, and more drill.

"Churchill said that battles are won by slaughter and manoeuvre,"

Andersson said. "The more a general contributes in manoeuvre, the less he demands in slaughter. As NCOs, the better you can manoeuvre men on the ground as cadets, the better you'll do it in the air as pilots."

When they weren't on the square, they were in the classroom, sketching out formations advancing in line and in columns, drawing crowns and chevrons to note the positions of sergeants, flight sergeants, warrant officers first and second class. Alex committed to memory the standard lengths of pace (thirty inches in quick and slow time, forty inches in double time), of steps out (thirty-three inches), steps short (twenty-one inches), and half paces (fifteen inches). Walking to and from the canteen or the latrine he counted out his cadences: 120 paces per minute in quick time, sixty in slow time, 180 paces per minute in double time. He sketched the exact radius of a left wheel (turning ninety degrees, one quarter of a circle having a radius of four feet, inner flank stepping short, outer stepping out, the squad dressing to the inner flank while keeping eyes front). He memorized passages from the *Manual of Drill and Ceremonial*. "The hallmarks of Canadian Forces drill are efficiency, precision, and dignity. These qualities are developed through self-discipline and practice. They lead to unit pride and cohesion." He said them like prayers as he lay in his bunk and the whoosh of vehicles on the Trans-Canada softly tore the stillness like afterburners in the distance.

MONEY THAT OTHER CADETS spent on chips, Cokes, and pinball, Alex spent on a model kit, a Monogram 1/32 scale Hawker Hurricane. Alex liked the Hurricane, he liked its stubby workhorse design, its fluted fabric sides that reminded you of the biplanes that came before it. This was the plane that really won the Battle of Britain, the plane that the highest scoring squadrons of Poles and Canadians flew while the Brits took all the credit in their slender Spitfires. It's the plane that he imagined himself flying alongside Skrebensky and Margate over the beaches of Normandy and the sands of Tobruk in the secret stories he made up for himself each night while he waited for sleep. He studied the instructions and gathered his tools: toothpicks to apply the glue, paintbrushes in three thicknesses, clothes pegs to use as clamps, and a table knife to heat and flatten bosses over landing gear hobs so that the wheels would actually turn. He broke the parts from away from their stanchions and scraped away excess plastic with a nail file.

"Hey Menkywitz. You ever actually gonna build that thing?"

McKnight set up on the table opposite him at the canteen, letting Horner and Margate do most of the work while he boasted about the virtues of his balsa wood P-40 Tomahawk, an expensive kit, one that would actually fly with its gas engine and radio control unit.

"Still shopping in the toy department, eh Menkywitz? You want to set your sights a little higher."

Alex argued that his Hurricane would look much more like the real thing when he was finished, with tan and olive drab camouflage on the wings and fuselage, duck-egg blue undersurfaces, and flesh tone and chrome yellow for the pilot's face and Mae West. To top it off, his kit had authentic decals for 303 Kościuszko Squadron, the first Polish fighter squadron to go operational in Britain. Whereas McKnight's P-40 was missing the Tomahawk's distinctive "Flying Tiger" markings and had ugly, inauthentic, black pistons sticking out of its cowling for the gas engine. The argument was lost on McKnight and, on the night Alex finally cemented the Hurry's wings into place, he was outside on the baseball diamond giving the Tomahawk its maiden flight. The model had just touched down when a cadet from an Oshawa squadron ran into the canteen shouting.

"You gotta see. Someone from the NCO course is streakin' the camp!"

Alex followed the cadet out to the main avenue just as a naked figure appeared from the direction of the shower tent, rolls of fat jiggling like soft cheese over his hips, hands clenched to his groin. He was pursued by a pack of cadets (Alex thought he saw Horner among them) brandishing tins of shaving cream, razors, and tubes and bottles of sundry solutions.

McKnight watched from the side of the diamond, turning a matchstick in his mouth as Margate packed away the P-40.

"McKnight. What's going on?"

McKnight didn't speak until the fleeing cadet turned in among the tents, showing the fan of purple acne on his back before he disappeared.

"It would seem," he said, "that Smelliot has finally got his masturbation papers."

"MARKER!" Margate marched straight at him, arms pumping to shoulder height like the pistons in a Rolls-Royce Merlin, and halted precisely three paces in front of him. Alex pivoted right, marched three paces and halted, pivoted left, and snapped to attention.

"SQUAD. FALL IN!"

Seventeen cadets, half the flight, strode across the square, dressed right on Margate, and shuffled into three ranks, leaving a neat gap in the centre rank — Elliot's position, now vacant in the wake of his withdrawal from the course.

"RI-YEET. TURN!"

Alex fought back the dryness in his mouth. He had already passed, with the highest mark in the course, the written drill test, a sketch diagram of the sequence he now had to execute on parade.

Lieutenant Andersson stood with Officer Cadet Burns in the shade at the edge of the square, clipboard at the ready to note every misstep, every botched command.

"Squad will advance in columns of three. By the left, QU-E-E-YI-CK, 'ARCH."

They set off, shoes slapping the pavement in perfect unison. Alex marched alongside them, swallowing back a flutter of panic, a disbelief that this machine was actually under his control. Calling the cadence settled his nerves.

"'EFT, 'EFT, 'EFT-'IGHT-'EFT-'IGHT, 'EFT, 'EFT."

Drill was music, with rhythms as sure as those applied with a ruler to the back of his hand by his piano teacher. The commands were a song in which Alex had found a voice. They rang out of him from a place he hadn't even known existed, somewhere behind his lungs. The squad responded almost before he gave the orders: left inclines, right inclines, open order, closed order, followed by an advance in line that broke into a hollow square whose sides he folded and unfolded as if they were the Duxford wing, performing Immelman turns, barrel rolls, and hammerheads in the skies of Essex. Alex drew the squad abreast of the Lieutenant and finished with a sharp salute. Andersson's equally sharp return of the salute told him that he'd bested the lot of them, including McKnight, who sulked in the shady background.

"L-A-C BL-I-I-NK-Y," HORNER CALLED from under his covers, where he'd been studying the July *Penthouse* by flashlight. "Are those your bed springs I hear squeaking?"

"Screw you, Horner." Skrebensky's comeback sounded awkward and unpractised.

"Screw me? I bet you'd really like that, wouldn't you Blinky?"

"Fuck off!"

"Leave him alone, Horner," said McKnight. "Blinky's got a heavy date."

"Yeah, with Hairy the Hand!"

"Why don't you lend him the mag, Horner? Help him speed things up so we can get some sleep."

"Nah. Miss July here would be wasted on him."

"Yeah, don't worry, Blinky. Someday your prince will come."

At reveille, Skrebensky's bunk was empty. Alex found him at the fence, fingers laced in the chain-link, staring across the Trans-Canada to the hangars that concealed the base's transports.

"Hey, Skreb."

Skrebensky didn't answer right away, just shuffled a little and blinked into the sun as it peaked over the control tower.

"We been here ten days and I haven't seen a single airplane. I seen more planes over my house in Toronto."

"Don't worry. We've got gliding on Friday. They won't cancel it this time."

"I won't be there."

"What do you mean?"

"I'm quitting."

"What, the course?"

"The course, camp, the squadron, everything."

Skrebensky shirt was untucked, his tie was loose and his shoes weren't tied. He had the same look about him as the little Scottish guy who goes wire crazy in *The Great Escape*.

"They're coming for me, Menk. I heard them planning it. They're gonna do to me what they did to Elliot."

"Why?"

"They know about the stockings. They know about what I asked you."

"Well, how did they find out?"

"I dunno. You tell me."

Skrebensky didn't fall in for mess parade. He didn't turn up for inspection, and when the Senior NCO course returned to barracks that evening, his kit was gone and his mattress stripped. It was almost nine o'clock when Alex finally got a minute alone in the tent with Margate.

"Did you tell McKnight what I told you?"

Margate smiled slyly at the shirt he was ironing. "About?"

"You know. The stocking. That thing he said to me."

"Well, you told me. It was a good story. I had to share it."

"Not with McKnight! He's a freakin' hyena."

"Well, hyenas've got to be fed, don't they? And better Skrebensky than one of us."

"But Skreb is one of us."

"He's queer as a three dollar bill. Can't have that around, can we?" Margate took up the immaculately pressed shirt he'd been ironing and laid it on McKnight's bunk, then he fixed Alex with a cold, crosshair stare.

"Unless, of course, you actually put that stocking on for him. Wouldn't want McKnight to know about that, now would we?"

"What is it with you and McKnight, anyway? You'd think it was you two who were — you know."

"You're such a kid, Menkywitz. You got no idea. McKnight may have been full of shit about his uncle being a fighter ace, but his dad is a wheel, a colonel at Defence HQ, a guy with pull. That's why Andersson lets him get away with murder. Andersson's been grounded for over a year because of something that happened when he was stationed at Summerside. He's desperate to get posted back to a squadron and McKnight's dad can make it happen. See, I'm not like you, Menkywitz. I actually got to think about my future and I've been studying how it all works. And it's not how you shine your shoes, or what you score on your drill test; it's who you know and who you blow. This is just a game of toy soldiers to you, but the forces, man, it's my future. It's my way outta Regent Park. I gotta do Senior Leaders after this. I gotta make warrant officer so I can get into the Royal Military College. McKnight's old man teaches there. Get the picture?"

A GREEN MONSTER JOSTLED them up a series of back roads on the scrubby flatlands north of the Lake Ontario shore, zigging and zagging until Alex had no idea where they were. Finally they pulled up to a set of iron gates where an elderly commissionaire sat watch. Lieutenant Andersson presented their orders and the gates squealed open, allowing the bus to continue down a dirt road in a cloud of late summer dust. The shells of abandoned hangars arched out of the stands of goldenrod ahead of them. Then a gasp sounded down the length of the bus.

"Holy shit, look at that!"

Ranged in the weeds behind the hangars were row upon row of mothballed jet fighters. Sabrejets, Canucks, Silver Stars stacked two and three high like Lincoln logs, landing gear of the upper rows resting on the wing roots of the lower ones. Their roundels were faded and their Perspex canopies had weathered to a milky white. Daylight shone through their tailpipes.

"It's like an elephant's graveyard," someone said.

The bus dropped them behind the hangars and Andersson marched them out to a tarmac sprouting ragweed between its concrete slabs. A cracked runway branched away from it and ran the length of the field. A glider sat tipped on its side at the runway's foot, the sun glinting on in its bone-white fuselage. A jeep emerged from one of the hangars, driven by a coveralled airman. It had a tarp pitched over the back half of its cab and a motorized winch with a large spool of cable bolted to the floor at its tailgate. Alex recognized the stocky officer in the jeep's passenger seat: Mr. Duczynski, a friend of his father's from the Air Force Association, an actual veteran of the Kościuszko Squadron. He was their pilot.

"They need a volunteer for the Jeep," said Andersson. "McKnight, roll up your sleeves, and go help Private Evans."

McKnight sauntered over to the vehicle which had stopped near the glider's nose, then began helping the aircraftsman unfurl the steel cable and attach it to a metal armature under the glider's nose cone. "Nice to see McKnight working for a change," Alex murmured to Margate.

"You kidding?" said Margate. "It's a reward. There's water on that truck, and shade."

Andersson announced that the flight would go up in alphabetical order. Anyone who tried to jump the queue would be washed out of the course. Then he said he was returning to the bus to do some paperwork and disappeared between the hangars.

Barclay, an LAC from Sudbury, was the first to go up, swinging himself over the lip of the glider's cockpit and buckling in next to Duczynski. The jeep nudged forward and the cable went taught. Then, on a hand signal from the pilot, the jeep plunged down the runway, the glider scurrying after it, silent except for the hum of its single tire on the concrete. Her ailerons dropped and she lifted into the air, rising to the full height her cable would allow. Then the cable fell away and the craft caught an updraft, rose another hundred feet, banked left, circled the field, and began a slow spiral down to the runway. She rolled to a stop at the same spot she had taxied from. Barclay got out and helped Beauchemin, the next cadet to go up, turn the crate into position for takeoff and the process was repeated with Bowden, Carter, Ciardelli, and Chouinard. Each cycle took about ten minutes to complete with each cadet averaging three minutes in the air. Alex ran through the flight roster in his head. He would have to wait at least an hour and a half for his turn.

By the time they got to Damiani, the heat was taking its toll on the waiting cadets, who squatted on the shadeless crabgrass at the edge of the tarmac. The windsock hung limp beside the runway and the cicadas buzzed like B-17s. Dark stains spread from their armpits, and their faces greased over with sweat that wouldn't evaporate in the humid air. After Dawes came down, McKnight strode over and said, "We need one more body on the jeep."

Immediately Horner, who'd been complaining more loudly than most about the heat, pulled himself to his feet, but McKnight pointed to Margate.

"C'mon Margate, lef' dat barge. Tote dat bale."

"What the fuck?" Horner protested weakly as McKnight and Margate retreated to the jeep's shaded cab and took hefty swigs from the water jug reserved for the crew. By Derzko's turn, watching the glider turn the same circuit had become as exciting as watching a Ferris wheel. Alex tried to picture the base as it must have been in wartime, a training field like the one his mother had worked on, buzzing with yellow Harvards, Ansons, and Gypsy Moths. But the heat had become blinding, even to his mind's eye.

Dwyer, Eaves, Edmonds. The cadets who'd been up began slipping away to find shade by the hangars.

"We should do the same, guys. It's too hot out here."

"Don't be a wimp, Minkywitz. Andersson said we should stay right here."

Elkington, Evgeni, Farrakhan. Alex loosened his tie, rolled down his knee socks. The others started doing the same, except for Horner who sat slumped forward on the ground, head between his knees.

"Horner?"

"Shit. My head."

Alex knelt in front of him, checked for the symptoms he'd been taught to look for in his St. John's Ambulance course: rapid breathing, the skin flushed but dry.

"Okay, he's got sunstroke. You two — Simone, Thomas." He took off his shirt. "Make some shade for him with this." He loosened Horner's tie and opened his shirt, then ran to the jeep, where Margate and McKnight lounged under their awning, and snatched up the water jug.

"Hey," McKight shouted after him. "That's for crew."

"Fuck off, McKnight."

Horner took a couple of slow sips and gasped as Alex lifted him in a fireman's carry and staggered toward the hangars, Simone following with the water. Once they had him in the shade Alex stripped Horner down to his shorts and gave him another drink.

"Keep giving him water," he told Simone, "but slowly. I'm going to look for Andersson."

He found the Lieutenant halfway up the road to the gate, contemplating the mothballed jets as if they were ciphers in a code he was trying to unscramble.

"You know this aircraft, Menkywitz?"

"CF-100 Canuck, sir."

"That's right. Just scrap now. They don't make wars like they used to."

"Sir ..." He gave Andersson a full account of Horner's condition and measures taken. The lieutenant slowly turned his attention away from the planes and studied Alex as if he were seeing him for the first time.

"You've done well, Menkywitz. I'll see to Horner. Get your shirt on and get back to the line. You don't want to miss your flight."

"Yes, sir." Alex saluted and turned to go.

"Oh, and Mienkiewicz."

"Sir?"

"You're a good kid, a true believer."

"Thank you, sir."

"I hope the world lets you down easy."

DUCZYNSKI, THE GLIDER PILOT, showed no sign of recognizing Alex when he buckled him into the passenger seat, and Alex made no mention of his father. The two sat in silence as the jeep edged away from them and the tow line went tight with the thump of a plucked bass string. The glider rumbled and fluttered as it pursued the jeep down the runway, then went silent as it rushed up to meet the clouds. They hung in the sky as if pinned there on the steel stem of the cable.

Duczynski turned to him and spoke through the rush of the air.

"See that lever beside your foot?"

"Yessir."

"Pull it."

He pulled, and they were free.

The Lesson

Miss Kalyn spins up the front walk, the kerchief tied tight over her head as if to keep it from flying off. The quick glances left and right, the sunglasses pressed high to the bridge of her nose, shoulders hunched to her earlobes; from her lookout post behind the front curtains, Marlene Mienkiewicz reads the piano teacher's body language and wonders what today's story will be. Miss Kalyn clutches an avocado purse to her side, so it won't be a repeat of the time she left her handbag on the Rexdale bus (the driver, acting on the orders of his superiors in the Masonic Lodge, had driven erratically in order to disorient her into leaving it on the seat). It could be another stalking incident involving the pianist Glenn Gould, who she believes has never forgiven her for almost defeating him at the Kiwanis Festival of 1944 and who retired from the concert stage in order to follow her around town in his car. Or she might have had another brush with the Mafia, of which she is convinced her Italian neighbour is a member.

Miss Kalyn stops at the door and waits without ringing because doorbells emit ultra-high frequencies that destroy the hearing.

"How do you do?" she says, as if she and Marlene were complete strangers, then brushes past into the dark hallway, ripening the air with her bad perfume. Miss Kalyn removes her kerchief, allowing tresses of unwashed brown hair to slide down to her shoulders. She does not remove the sunglasses.

"Tell me, Mrs. Mienkiewicz," she asks with a nod to the front door. "Do you see a Muskox outside?"

Marlene goes back to the door and peeks through the sheers.

"I'm sorry, Miss Kalyn. I'm afraid I don't quite know what you're looking for."

"A Muskox. Those cars that all the hooligans are driving."

"You mean Mustangs?"

"Yes. Those. I'm sure one of them has been following me. All the way from Mississauga."

"I don't see one."

"You can't see from there. You must go outside and look."

Marlene goes outside and looks. No Mustangs, just the bulky Oldsmobiles and Buicks favoured by the factory workers who live on Galway Avenue. Marlene can't believe she's doing this. Across the street, Mrs. Schwilpo glances up from the carpet she is beating over her porch railing and fixes Marlene with a squint. Mrs. Schwilpo dismissed Miss Kalyn as her kids' piano teacher long ago. So did all the other families who had engaged her. Now everyone is waiting for Marlene to do the same.

"There's nothing," she says as she steps back inside. "Nothing unusual, just our neighbours' cars." A tremor passes over Miss Kalyn's features. Her lips purse and release in a hint of the concert hall smile that once graced the stages of Warsaw, Kraków, and Prague. Reassured, she is ready to begin.

Marlene knots her hands in her apron and looks for somewhere to look.

"Alex is late again," she lies.

"Your son makes a habit of this lateness, Mrs. Mienkiewicz."

A sly timbre colours Miss Kalyn's voice. She understands this exercise, has worked through its steps many times.

"Alex is a busy boy. He's on the student council, he's in a play, he has his sports ..."

"*Un jeune homme engagé.* So like his father. I understand. But you must teach Alex to set his priorities," Miss Kalyn instructs her. "You must be firm."

"Yes, of course, Miss Kalyn. You're right."

Miss Kalyn sweeps into the front room and lights on her usual chair beside the piano.

"Well?" Miss Kalyn prompts. "Shall we begin with Blaise, then?"

"Of course. Blaise."

It's a long trudge up to the landing outside her younger son's third floor room. The poster on his door asks "Suppose They Gave a War and Nobody Came?" and its Day-Glo festoons make her dizzy when she stands too close. She clears her throat, giving the boy an extra second's warning so he can spirit away anything she might not care to see, then knocks.

"Yup," he calls. She pushes open the door. Blaise slouches in the beanbag chair by the window. His legs, sheathed in flares of purple corduroy, extend to the window sill where his clunky shoes bob to the music thudding in the speakers on either side of him. At his side is a large juice tin filled with yellow sand. The statue of the Blessed Virgin he was given for his first communion is planted head down in the sand, the rim of its inverted base smudged with nicotine stains.

Say nothing, she tells herself. Say nothing about the statue. Say nothing about the cigarette butts that she knows are buried in the tin. Say nothing about the briny male odour that permeates the room. Say nothing about the comic books and music magazines overlaying the untouched homework on his desk. Say nothing about anything and maybe her son, her baby, will do this one little thing. For her sake.

"Miss Kalyn is here, Blaise."

"How come? We're not taking lessons anymore. Dad said."

"I know. But — well — she's here, so. Perhaps, we could just humour her a bit longer?"

Blaise cranes around the back of his chair, his features pointed with mischief under the fall of his long shag cut.

"Mum, this is so telepathetic it skittishicizes me!"

The boy pauses to savour the bewilderment his school chums' private vocabulary causes her. Then he draws himself forward as the reality of the situation dawns on him.

"You haven't told her! You still paying her?"

"Yes."

"With what? Dad's not giving you the money anymore."

"We can't just brush her off, Blaise. She's a distinguished pianist."

"She's a head case."

"You're the only students she has left. She needs the support of her community."

"Since when are *we* the community? We don't even speak Polish. You know what the community's doing? They're laughing at us 'cause we're the only ones who'll let her in the house."

Marlene points to the photo hanging over his bed.

"Miss Kalyn was good enough for him, the piano player in that band you're so crazy about."

"Nicki Bury? You can't even ask her about it. She just freaks when you say his name."

True. Miss Kalyn sees the success of her famous pupil as a personal humiliation.

"Hey Mom, I got an idea. Why don't you take the lessons?"

"Me? Don't be ridiculous."

"Okay, so you gonna pay just to listen to her loony speeches? How long you gonna let it go on?" Blaise asks with a pimply leer.

Back on the landing, Marlene pauses and tries to reconcile the young cynic in the beanbag chair with the white-blond toddler who loved trains and wept when she hung his stuffies on the line to dry after he took them swimming in his splashpool. "How did this happen?" she wonders. "How have I ended up so alone?"

She finds Miss Kalyn at the front window, scanning the street for Mustangs.

"I'm afraid Blaise isn't feeling well again," she says. "He won't be down."

The piano teacher seems not to hear. She keeps her eyes to the street. Striking eyes. Green, tinged with flecks of gold. If only she'd learn how to apply her eyeliner.

"Alex shouldn't be long. I'll make some tea."

Marlene retreats to her kitchen. The vegetables lie unpeeled on the counter. Thad will just have to wait for his dinner tonight, even if it makes him late for his evening shift at the Parish Trust (or for the Air Force Association, the Legion or some pensioner whose taxes he's agreed to do). It's him who started this. Why isn't he here to finish it? The bump and scrape of furniture in the front room tells her that Miss Kalyn is once again rearranging the furniture around the piano — to correct the dissonances in the room's acoustics.

"So that's where she got to!" said Liz Hejnal, Thad's assistant at the Trust, when someone mentioned that Zosia Kalyn was giving piano lessons. Liz had been in St. Bolesław's choir when Miss Kalyn was the church organist. "They thought they were a cut above everyone else," she said. "The whole fandamily."

Liz told them how Miss Kalyn's parents came as political refugees before the war, which meant they had to have been communists. The father spent all his time in the greasy spoons on Copernicus Avenue, holding forth as if he were still in the cafés of Warsaw while his wife worked shifts at Dempster's bakery. Liz said that Zosia was an obvious talent from the get-go and nothing was good enough around St. Bolesław's. She won all the competitions, topped her class at the conservatory, almost beat out Glenn Gould at the Kiwanis.

Then she was discovered by Alloysius Ardaszkiewicz, the pianist and hero of the resistance. Marlene saw him at Massey Hall with Thadeus on one of their first dates. They were introduced to him at the reception afterwards, the shock of white hair swept back from his temples, fingers still hot from the performance as he took up her hand to kiss it. After that tour, he spirited Miss Kalyn off to Warsaw at the age of seventeen.

"The old goat," said Liz. "Him in his sixties, and her barely finished convent school. He takes her back to Poland, tutors her, gives her the big buildup, and then, on the eve of her first big concert tour, he croaks. A stroke, though Zosia's dad swore up and down Copernicus Avenue that he'd been poisoned. Who knows? The old boy had enemies for sure, and once he was gone, the knives came out for Zosia. The official critics dumped all over her. That's when she went off the deep end."

And now it was this: the long bus rides in from Mississauga, students who despised her, and parents who catalogued her eccentricities to fuel the firestorm of gossip that followed her around the neighbourhood.

"Like letting a wild animal into your house," said the mother of one former pupil as they stood in line outside the Crippled Civilians store one Thursday morning.

Miss Kalyn comes into the kitchen clutching the windup clock that belonged to Marlene's great aunt Lex.

"Mrs. Mienkiewicz, you must never, never leave such items on your piano."

"But Miss Kalyn. It's not electrical."

"All the same, Mrs. Mienkiewicz. It is metallic and invites the possibility of fields which could magnetize your piano."

Marlene plucks the clock from Miss Kalyn's grip and says, "I will try to remember that." Marlene learned early on that the room with the piano had to be cleared of electrical devices. The record player, the adding machine, and the old tube radio that was a wedding present all had to find new homes. Thadeus's rolltop desk had to be locked after Miss Kalyn was caught going through it looking for paper clips, staplers, rulers, and any other metal objects that might cause an unwelcome vibration during a lesson.

While the tea brews, Marlene steals a glance into the front room to monitor the progress of the inspection, but the teacher has suspended her search. She stands at the old upright, her hands resting on keys that are yellowed and chipped. The fingertips flutter and twitch but don't produce a sound. Marlene has only heard Miss Kalyn play once, two years ago, when, frustrated with Alex's slow progress on a Chopin prelude, she shoved him aside and launched into a rendition of the composer's *Etude in C Minor*.

"You see, Alex," she crooned as she played. "See how the chords in the treble modulate through the dominant till they reach the subtonic, how they surprise us, how they bound even further up, all the time resisting these arpeggios plunging downwards in the bass. Now the theme, always thrusting at the upper registers. It is the eagle weaving in a sky red with its own blood, major tearing at minor, it is longing and it is defiance. This is your history, Alex. It is who you are. There is no escape. Defeat is inevitable, but hear the great things we make of it!"

The women of Galway Avenue, the ones who have banished her from their homes, say Miss Kalyn refuses to play in front of her pupils because she has "lost her touch." Marlene knows otherwise.

"The music doesn't lie," she told Alex once. "Never waste it on people who do."

Maybe that's why Marlene lets the charade continue. Maybe she can't accept that the music has been wasted on her.

"The tea is made," she says, setting the tray down on the coffee table.

Marlene pours into two of the bell-shaped Blue Willow cups she collected from the junk stores on Queen Street, then sits opposite Miss Kalyn, who perches on the edge of the sofa and stares into the middle distance as if someone were holding up a score for her to read. There is nothing you can ask this woman. She doesn't cook, clean, shop, sew, or knit. She has no children, no husband, no house, nothing that harmonizes with Marlene's experience. So Marlene just sips the tea that she has learned to drink in the Polish style, very clear with lemon, and hopes for a story about Warsaw stirring itself out of the rubble, of the old people sitting among the roses that ring Chopin's rebuilt statue, eyes closed, as if hearing his music on the breeze.

Instead, Miss Kalyn's eyes focus on the bookshelf and she sets down her tea with a clatter. She crosses the room, skirts swiping at the furniture, and snatches up a record sleeve. Glenn Gould standing on the ice at Lake Simcoe.

"Mrs. Mienkiewicz. Surely you haven't gone over to *Gould?*"

"It's really very good," says Marlene, who checks herself from adding that it was only a quarter at Aberdeen Antiques.

"This!" cries the piano teacher, shaking the sleeve illustration of the muffled little man on the ice. "This is treachery indeed. This is not music. It's just wheels and gears. It is the clock on your piano, Mrs. Mienkiewicz. It is machinery where it has no business being! Gould will suck the air from your boys' playing, Mrs. Mienkiewicz. He is one of those cats who crawls into beds and steals the breath of children!"

She's off, arms circling as she conducts her resentment.

"They loved him in Russia, you know. Your Gould. They gave him flowers. These mechanical men. These theorists! Gould has no idea what he is playing at. He is still a child in his shorty pants."

Miss Kalyn waves aside a plate of the sugar cookies baked just this morning. From the avocado handbag, she extracts the watch that she never wears on her wrist, holds it at a safe distance to consult it, and says, "I am sorry Mrs. Mienkiewicz, but it would appear that your boys have once again missed their lessons."

As if he had been clocking the hour, Blaise turns his stereo up so that a bass line shudders down the staircase.

"Ha!" Miss Kalyn huffs. "So your son has also learned to hide behind his machinery. A real Gould! This rock and roll, it is nothing but a logical extension, I tell you. Machine music. Yes, a logical extension."

She re-fastens her kerchief and returns the sunglasses to the bridge of her nose. In the front hall she turns smartly to Marlene as if to deliver an encore.

"You must remind Alex how to think of his pieces," she says. "He must round his shoulders like a bear in the Liszt. In the Prokofiev, he must rummage among prickly thorns. For the Bach, especially in the *rubato*, he must remember what the courtier says to the lady-in-waiting. Everywhere he must make flutes of his arms and flames of his fingers."

Marlene goes into the kitchen, opens the drawer where she keeps the housekeeping money, and makes a quick calculation. If she serves hamburger instead of lamb chops, Tang instead of orange juice, stretches the Sunday roast to two dinners and mixes more powdered skim into the two percent, she can just manage the ten dollars.

"I should not be taking it," says Miss Kalyn. "You must tell Mr. Mienkiewicz he is very generous."

Marlene steps onto the porch and watches the piano teacher spin down the walk as furiously as she came. Yes, she thinks, Thadeus will be angry when he finds out, but, after he has come and gone and she is alone, it will have all been worth it, just so she can call her sister M-K and tell her all about Muskoxes and Gould and what it means to have flutes for arms and flames for fingers.

Twelve Versions of Lech

I still look up to Lech's second floor window whenever I pass. During those times when he wouldn't answer the door, he'd be there, perched over the street, chin in hand, staring down the gargoyles of St. Voytek's church. On Sundays I'd look up guiltily as I slunk out of mass behind my parents and I could see him framed in the bay window, my judge and saviour, improbably balanced on the back of a chair.

A BIG MAN IN neutral clothes, trousers held up with rope and hair like an overturned stork's nest. Lech extended a broad hand and asked, "Does your father smoke a pipe?"

"Why yes," I said. "He does."

And then Lech just walked away before I could shake with him.

Yola Skarpinski, proprietor of the neighbourhood's only bookstore, had prepared his way. She told us about Lech's canvasses and prints hanging in the Prado, at MoMA, and in the Pompidou. She told us how Magritte helped him defect after he won the 1962 biennale in Brussels. An artist was loose on Copernicus Avenue, the real thing. He was the kind of artist our parents were certain not to like, an escape artist who had given gravity the slip.

"WHEN YOU GET DOWN to nothing, that's when you got something."

The emptiness of Lech's flat could make your head spin. The smell of dust baking on iron radiators. No bedroom. No backrests on any of the chairs except the one that sat in the front window. CBC programs murmured from a clock radio twenty-four hours a day, backed by the click of mechanical digits flipping over every sixty seconds. Sills and doorjambs sagged under the weight of paint.

By the telephone, a plastic cup shaped like Jiminy Cricket, with eyes that followed you as you inspected his prints. *Objects at the Speed of Nothing*, he called them, swaths of cool colour sweeping over one another. They were expressions of reductionism, which was an advancement, he claimed, on the anti-velocitarian movement he founded in Kraków in the fifties. The anti-velocitarians would paint themselves white then lie in groups of twenty across the lengths of canvas on which the art college forced them to paint portrait after identical portrait of Stalin. They staged "manifestations of immobility" to block major intersections, market squares and the forecourts of state enterprises. They incited workers to acts of stillness with instruction cards printed in letters so small that the police couldn't read them. Neither, of course, could the workers.

"So," Lech concluded, eyes gleaming with mischief, "Anti-velocitarianism accomplished exactly nothing. That was a great, great success!"

HE WAS A FABULOUS liar and, to prove it, he threw himself down on a park bench next to an American couple perspiring cheerfully into identical wool suits.

After some pleasantries about the hot Canadian summer that the Americans had not expected, the husband leaned confidentially into Lech and said, "You're not from around here, are you?"

Lech raised his hands in surrender. "And how do you know that?"

"Oh, I can tell by your accent," the American chuckled. "You're one of those French-Canadians, aren't you?"

"Actually no. You are wrong."

"I am? Then what are you?"

"I," Lech announced, "am a Laplander."

The American nodded as if a nagging doubt had been solved at last. His wife laid a hand on Lech's knee.

"I've always wondered," she said. "Do you people pay income tax?"

"We do," Lech confided. "We pay it in bones."

"HERE."

It was a black and white glossy snapshot, edges serrated like a postage stamp. Lech's hair was pure black and has yet to thin at the crown. His grin was softened with awe as it faced the unmistakable mustachios and mad stare of the elderly man across the café table from him: Dali.

"This is taken the day before Dali got me my refugee status in Barcelona. He spoke no Polish, I spoke no Catalan, so I looked at him across the table and said in English, 'Does your father smoke a pipe?'"

Was it Dali or Magritte? Barcelona or Brussels? And was it true that he had married his way into Canada and had a wife and daughter in Montreal? What about his family in Poland? Weren't there consequences back then for the relatives of defectors?

Rumours seeped through the footings of all his relationships. We wanted more. We wanted facts, a truth we could trust, and to be trusted, as equals, with the truth. But if you pressed Lech too hard you risked banishment.

"Journalist!" he would hiss. And you'd be banished for weeks to the sidewalk below his window.

YOLA SKARPINSKI SERVED TEA among her unsold copies of Gide and Zola while we talked, as always, about Lech.

"Has he told you," she asked, "about the day he came home from school and found all his neighbours hanging from lamp posts?"

Nobody spoke.

"Is that true?" I asked.

Yola smiled as she screwed a Sobranie into her amber cigarette holder. "It's not my place to say. You will never know what really happened to Lech or any of us. We mean nothing by it, darling. It is a silent agreement we all have with ourselves, that nothing will ever make us prisoners again, not even a memory."

"GO GET US SOME nice cake."

He said it as if we had been arguing about cake for years. I took his twenty dollar bill, went to Pani Wysotska's bakery and bought a cheesecake. Something was up. Lately he had been setting more than the usual number of loyalty tests, pranks meant to drive us away. A week earlier, while they argued about the validity of society as poetical concept, Lech had served my brother Blaise multiple shots of *spiritus* in glasses of herb tea with honey. Lech said this was the traditional way to drink *spiritus* in his part of Poland. The tea turned out to be a laxative.

When I brought the cheesecake back to Lech, he stared at the ten-inch slab in disbelief. Wordlessly he went to the kitchen, came back with a fork, and handed it to me along with the cake box.

"You bought that whole thing!" he said. "So now you gonna eat that whole thing!"

I stopped my throat with creamy curds until I was too heavy to lift myself.

I would have eaten fifty cakes that afternoon. Just to show him.

HE LIKED TO WATCH the phone ring until the caller gave up, then make bad jokes about who it might have been: a trunk call from Hannibal and his elephants, Richard Nixon inviting us to a taping, Leonid Brezhnev using a Party line.

"But what if it's something important?" I asked him once.

He just looked at me as if I'd lost my mind.

The longest time I ever saw him on the phone he didn't say a word. He sat on the floor with his eyes closed as if he were conducting the caller's voice into the shag carpet through his limp appendages. Then he turned the receiver into the room so that I could hear the woman's voice meandering inside it. She spoke Polish, soft runs of consonants, cadences of heartbreak that the language frames so well. Lech let me hear every word as the woman bared her soul in the tongue I had grown up surrounded by and still didn't understand.

After she had hung up he said, "Aleksei, the artist must be completely selfish."

LECH KISSED THERESE'S HAND in the manner of my father's generation and said, "So Aleksei, I finally meet your attachment."

Then he thrust a folio of his *InAction* lithographs at her as if he was serving a summons. Hugging the folio, Therese retreated to the window over the street, to the chair with the back on it, where no one but Lech ever sat. Lech stayed in the kitchen the whole time, scrubbing plates that never left the sink with a two-bit-sized scouring pad with the same ferocity I remembered Therese attacking Pani Zielinska's famous pot. The harder he scrubbed, the longer Therese took to pour over the lithographs. She sat with legs crossed, the free foot jiggled impatiently the way it still does whenever she's forced to suffer fools. Finally she brought the folio back to the kitchen and set it in the drying rack saying, "Have you ever drawn a baby? Or an apple?"

"I HAVE DEVISED A spectacle for you and your beautiful young lady," he said. "It is called The Spectacle of Adam and Eve. There will be a beautiful music and chanting. We will fill the room with incense. Then you and your young lady will come to the stage. You will remove each other's clothes, cover yourselves in oils, and make beautiful love. And we gonna do that in the church hall of the St. Voytek's! Now how about that?"

"Sure, Lech."

I humoured him for a whole month as he regaled me with plans for the lighting, sets, and music. Then I panicked when he showed me a signed contract for the hall.

"I'm not going through with it, Lech. I — I just can't."

Lech smiled his little smile and put a hand on my shoulder.

"So. Now we know," he said.

SOME LUNATIC HAD SHOT the Pope. Within hours of the shooting, the ground in front of his statue at the entrance to the Parish Trust was littered with flowers. I bought a single carnation and was furtively laying it on the pile when Lech emerged from the Trust office clutching a hydro bill in his left hand. The hand skittered behind his back, as if he were embarrassed to be caught doing something as mundane as paying a bill. But he recovered when he realized what I was doing and recognized his philosophical advantage.

"Does this bother you, what has happened to *Il Papa?*"

"Of course," I said. "Doesn't it bother you?"

"Why should it? They always kill the popes. Haven't you heard of Luc-r-r-r-ezia Borgia? She poisoned three of them. Her brothers!"

"But today ..."

"Aha! You think because today we have garbage disposal and air conditioning this will not happen. Come on. I show you something."

Lech steered me down the length of Copernicus Avenue, bobbing among shoppers moored to the boxes of fruit and cheap underwear in front of the shops. We reached the bottom of the street where it widens into a multi-veined delta of streetcar tracks. At first, I thought he was taking me to the Katyn monument, but he brushed past the cleft bronze monolith with its candles dissolving in the sun. The Sunnyside Bridge vaulted us toward the blue skies over Lake Ontario, then set us down outside the Palais Royale. Around back of the old dance hall, on the sand at the water's edge, Lech stretched out his arms and offered himself to the place where the blue of the water met the blue of the air.

"Did you know Austrian was the first language of Kanada?"

"No."

"Yes. Do you know what the Indians said — in Austrian — when your Jacques Cartier asked what was the name of this place?"

"Canada."

"Exactly. Ka-na-da. And in Austrian this means *Keine dar* — 'nobody's there.'"

"I thought it meant 'village of small huts' or 'swamp' or something."

"No, you are wrong. Because nobody thought about asking what those words mean until after they killed all the Indians with the smallpox. What you think about that? You live in a country where nobody knows what its name means. Do you read your great Canadian critics of literature?"

"No."

Lech swelled with pleasure at this lapse in my scholarship.

"They say the great question for you is 'Where is here?' So now you got the answer to that question. The Indians give it you. You know where is here?"

"No, Lech. Why don't you tell me where is here?"

"Here," he said, "is nowhere. And that, Aleksei, is a good, good place to be."

He turned to the lake and sang out in his roisterous baritone.

"KA-NA-DA."

I followed his gaze to the vanishing point where, for the first time, I saw the inspiration for his *Objects at the Speed of Nothing*. I saw how the void had beckoned to him in a world murderous with ideas. Lech waded into the algae-clotted shallows my mother had always warned us about, his untucked shirt billowing like a sail. As I watched his reflection scatter in the surf, I felt anchored and old. At the same time I realized that, no matter how old we felt, I and all the spiritual expeditionists of Copernicus Avenue were still too young for the world that Lech had known.

We probably always would be.

Gorky

The yard is a ruin. Stunted shoots of wheat, barley, and rye fringe gutters and shattered sills. Frozen stalks poke upwards between the ties of the railway siding next to the feed plant. Everywhere, gangways and eaves are bearded with a yellow-grey mixture of grain dust and pigeon droppings.

The last trucks snort up to chutes that dangle down the silos' backsides and ton upon ton of Canada Grade A pours into their hoppers. Men probe the loads with long sounding rods, while the yard foreman walks from cab to cab, a clipboard wedged in his artificial hand, checking waybills, and avoiding brawls.

Night draws over like a tarp. Inside the mill, bulbs cast their webbed light on an emptiness of bins, and on sixteen men in a shed.

When the full-timers change shift, sixteen men can seem like a thousand as they clatter and curse at their lockers.

"Hey boys. You hear it? Is coming corn boat."

Casey likes to leave the door open and talk when he's in the shower, the better to draw the younger men's attention to his tortured nakedness. There's a hunch in his right shoulder, the blade sticking straight out like a folded wing. Three fingers on his right hand are missing, and two deep fissures make a St. Andrew's cross in the middle of his chest. It happened twenty years ago when Casey was trying to free a crowbar that had got sucked up into the leg.

Bones, chairman of the bike gang, slams in from the pier and notices his lieutenant, Deano, reading the newspaper.

"Hey Deano. What the fuck you doin', man? You can't read."

Deano seeks refuge in the bikini-line on page three.

"Fuck off. I can read."

"Oh yeah? Then read me sumfin'. Here. Read me this here."

"I don't gotta' prove nuthin' to you."

"Ha! See? What a faggot. Sits there with a newspaper in front of him and he can't even fuckin' read."

"Fuck off."

"Hey Deano. Don't feel bad. Lotsa people got your problem. It's nothing to be ashamed of. Hey! You know what? You should take one of those night courses they got for people like you."

"I can fuckin' read."

"Take a fuckin' night course!"

Bones plunges on into the crypt, an anteroom where Abou Nidal, the Palestinian, conducts his combustible card games.

"I fold."

"Like fuck you fold."

"I said I fold, *madon*."

"Fuck you then."

There is a crash, then Abou's voice, smooth as humus.

"Gentlemen gentlemen, please, your bets."

At a table furrowed with initials and obscenities, Blaise feigns concentration on a book of poems by Rimbaud. His reading habits have deteriorated since his first days here. The hash doesn't help. It was impossible to resist an offer of the fine blond stuff that the war in Lebanon has made impossible to get — unless, like Abou, you have the right connections.

"First my family was in Lebanon," he likes to explain. "Then the Israelis chase us from there. So we go to Kuwait. The CIA chase us from there. Now I hide here. I was in business painting houses. But my partner was a Jew and I was stealing from him and he was stealing from me and so we went bankrupt. They are smart people the Jews. It is too bad we must kill each other because we have all been so stupid."

The dope is still buzzing in Blaise's thighs and armpits, so he reaches for the newspaper and succumbs to page three.

"Cindy is all wet for water sports and horseback riding."

"Hoo lookee her. Cheese gotterussy in a roontag."

Lenny is a walking artillery shell primed with septuagenarian lechery. The mill has tried to retire him several times but he keeps coming back.

"Cheese noffer you, bye. Yer bedder keepin' a pocket pussy."

He tosses down a perfectly formed rubber pudendum for Blaise's delectation. It is shaded all the right colours and has black nylon hair and a long penile gangway extending from the vagina.

"Call ease cow in pocket pussy. Pecherly w'licorice saliva."

Lenny snatches back the pocket pussy and goes to his locker, redirecting the monologue at his neighbour, Marek.

"Chow bead yer licorice saliva. W'llem horse is godit in archangels."

Marek blinks at the holy cards that line his locker door, adjusts his glasses, and returns to his inventory. Marek is the maintenance man and has a shed of his own; the locker is strictly a business address. He appears at regular intervals to dispense cans of Coke, cigarettes, chocolate and newspapers, all at cut-rate prices. He says little, but the other Poles speak of him with hushed reverence.

"He good fixet up guy," Casey told Blaise once. "Marek, he makin' bamps."

"Bombs?"

"Yeah, bamps. In war he makin' miney, he makin' grenadey. All kinds bamps!"

Marek picked up his mechanical know-how as an explosives expert during the uprising in Warsaw. Blaise has seen the fabulous stash of cigarettes and chocolate in his shed — old habits dying hard.

Fat Freddy wheezes into position on the other side of the table and pours a slug of tea from the Thermos that everyone knows he has kept spiked with vodka ever since his wife died. Blaise doesn't let on that he remembers Borżena from when they lived on Galway up Copernicus Avenue.

Gerald, the most celebrated drunk among the unloaders, staggers up from the crypt.

"Hey Freddy. You ever been to Gurky."

"Sure. Heh-heh. Polski Ogórki!"

"No, no, no. I mean that real Gurky they gots in the Soviet Union."

"I no go Sovietsky. I Germany."

"Oh-h that's too bad because I-I'd really like to know about Gurky. I understan' they gots quite a cistern."

Marek goes to the new kid who's been sulking on a stool just outside the crypt. He gives the kid a Pepsi, a pack of Export A's, and an Aero bar, then goes. "They say in Gurky that's where they send all the people what thinks —"

The kid tears greedily into the chocolate, looking up with the quick furtive glances of a stray.

"It's a city full of sensitive souls and axe murders."

The kid is wearing a tie, polished platform shoes, a maxi-coat and bell bottoms that bell halfway up his shins.

"I heared that, in Gurky, it's possible to eat death. I never been to Gurky, but I seen it in dreams."

The kid looks at Blaise and smiles a chocolate smile that has dog meat written all over it.

"Repeat after me," Blaise says to Blaise. "I am not my brother's keeper. I am not my brother's keeper."

Lenny and Fat Freddy begin to argue.

"You go nowhere, Lenny. You stay here workin' you whole life, you lazy fuck!"

"Hooyoo haulin' azey you sumbitchcocksuckhole. I heave this chittole soozyme fuckin a lyre!"

Bones snatches Cindy out of Blaise's hands.

"No wonder chicks get raped."

"Yep. No place like Gurky."

"You fucker die here."

Blaise escapes onto the pier, which is walled in by the ulcerated hull of the *Beacon of Enterprise*. The ship is a seven-hundred-foot laker, with cabins fore and aft. She was saved from the scrapyards two years ago by Shamrock Shipping of Port Colborne to ply the last regular run into this mill from the Lakehead. As the leg sucks up her cargo, the *Beacon* lists in toward the silos, as if for protection.

Blaise trudges toward the portal of daylight out past her stern, slowed by the extra pounds of wheat in his jacket lining and the half-frozen matrix of mud and spilt seed that sucks at his boots. At the end of the pier he kicks the bloated corpse of a rat into the water and seats himself on a mooring stanchion.

His thoughts are a confusion of Polish voices and fractured machinery. But the mill's immensity acts as a shield from the city and the rush of the expressway. The harbour is perfectly still with ice that is whiter than anything in this lake deserves to be. And the jade green tugboat channels are widening with each passing week to offer a landing place for mergansers and golden eyes. Last year there were loons for a few days. No one in the city heard their cries but him. That's Blaise's first vanity, to think he's the only one who sees and hears anything in the waterfront's secret places.

He wants the foreman's buzzer to keep him from looking back into the riot of himself. He takes off the ring his father brought back for him from a pilgrimage to Spain, with its gold inlay of Don Quixote tilting at windmills, and stows it in his pocket. Once they're in the hold, his muscles will wring themselves out in the delight of battering iron, and he'll be able to stop pondering his second and much greater vanity, the belief that you can only find beauty in ruins, that things this brutal are the only things you can really call true.

In Transit

Therese had offered to take Blaise to one of the Queen Street cafés where all the types went. But he had insisted on the coffee shop in Union Station's Great Hall, and so here she was, sweating through her shoulder pads and smoking again while Blaise played with the croutons in a bowl of French onion soup. The peak of his floppy checked cap almost touched the tip of his nose and a soup-stained napkin billowed up to his chin, rendering him faceless. Therese tried to entertain him with light conversation.

"So Susan asked me if Alex is gay and I said to her, 'No, but most of the good ones are.'"

Blaise chopped a crouton in half, smiled, and pressed his knees tightly together beneath the table. Therese turned her attention to an unattended child eating spaghetti with its fingers two tables over. What had she been thinking, offering to meet like this? What miraculous powers did she think she possessed? Ridiculous to think she could bridge this gap. Neither brother was going to be moved by her attempt to reconcile them. Alex would be furious if he knew she was here, and Blaise was doing his best to bring out the worst in her. She took a deep drag on her cigarette and sent a jet of smoke into the shadow that hid his face.

Blaise pushed his cap back and removed the napkin from the collar of his shirt. The shirt was actually a pyjama top which went rather well, in an offbeat way, with the Harris tweed jacket his mom had scooped for him at the Crippled Civilians. All through the seventies, in high school and into university, Blaise had been the embodiment of Bohemian chic, ingeniously bending the St. John's College dress code, exchanging his grey flannels and blue blazer for Indian tops and wide wail cords the minute he left the school grounds. Now the castoff look he'd picked up at art school was beginning to date. His fair hair, reddish, like his mom's, broke in greasy strings at his shoulders, a length that was rapidly ceasing to be fashionable on guys. He looked like someone whom the world was leaving behind, skin beginning to sag under the fine pointed jawline he had inherited from his father. There were dark circles under his eyes, though his gaze was as sharp as ever when he snatched up the pencil and sketchpad he still carried with him.

"So Treese, how are the wedding plans coming?"

His tone said it all; so, just to spite him, she told him everything he didn't want to know, how their parents had St. Voytek's booked less than an hour after she and Alex had announced the engagement. The catering was a given too, of course, Gołąbki, pierogi, patyczki, and roast chicken provided by Pani Jastrszak, with desserts from Madame Wysotska's. More guests than they would have liked, but they'd been surprised by the number of out-of-town guests who said they'd come: her uncle and aunt from Edmonton, his cousins from Chicago, there was even talk of a cousin or two coming from Poland.

This rendezvous with Blaise made her wedding plans seem an exercise in happy forgetfulness. She pulled out her quilted Chanel bag with gold chain and rummaged through an assortment of vials, tubes, and brushes, a mini-pack of Finger Pinkies, a crumpled Law Society bulletin, her Filofax, and a plastic folder containing her baby pictures. At the very bottom, she found a file and proceeded to work at a hangnail as she expanded on the table decorations for the hall, reading selections, seating arrangements, and, most important, the music.

"We were hoping you could help us with that, Blaise. No punk music, though. No Buzzcocks, no Sex Pistols. Blaise? Blaise!"

Blaise wasn't listening. He had laid his head on the table to get a better look at the ceiling details of the station's Great Hall, his pencil scratching furiously on the pad in front of his nose, like a kid on a carpet with a colouring book.

"Blaise, what in hell are you doing?"

"Huh?" Blaise jerked upright and snatched up his fork. "I was just looking at the ceiling."

"What for?"

"Plotting an escape."

He winked and pulled his cap back down over his eyes.

"Will you please take off that cap."

"Can't." He beckoned her closer and whispered. "It's part of my disguise. I only take it off when there's no danger of being recognized."

"Escape? Disguises?" Therese pressed her lips tight in reproof. "Blaise, we are not little kids and this isn't High Park."

"Aha! *So you seenk you have vays of makingk me talk!*"

While Therese pondered what he could possibly mean, Blaise leaned back in his chair and, with a flourish, lit the wrong end of a cigarette.

"Blaise!" He shot forward in his seat and spat the flaming cigarette into his onion soup. When Therese laughed in spite of herself, he picked up her silver-plated lighter and held it over the bowl.

"Oops."

Blaise let it slip with a plop that spattered the tabletop with a column of broth.

"Sorry," he offered unconvincingly. "I'm such a klutz."

Therese plucked the lighter from its bed of molten mozzarella and held it pinched between bright magenta nails while Blaise fidgeted with the ring on his finger.

"You prick."

"You bring out the best in me, baby."

She could have left right then and there, but that's what he wanted, and she wasn't about to give it to him. Contempt for his and respect for her own sheer bloody-mindedness kept her jabbing at errant cuticles while he returned to studying the ceiling of the Great Hall where the announcer heralded the arrival of a train from Vancouver that had passed through Calgary, Regina, Winnipeg, and Thunder Bay.

"Your family are managing. Thanks for asking."

Blaise, only semi-present as he watched a tide of arrivals dash itself against the departures clock and then subside in eddies of cloth and clicking shoe leather, huffed in soundless derision.

"They'd really like to know how you're making out with the treatment."

No answer but the urgent gratings of his pencil on the sketchpad. Therese leaned over to study his creation, a web of fragments, architecturals, geometrics, battering one another across the page, hats, shoes, and wallets cascading down white cones of light toward a clock face bereft of hands. A few stickish figures knelt below the clock with suitcases and backpacks, itineraries lifted in front of their faces like breviaries, rosaries sketched round their wrists.

"What do they make you do, anyway? Why don't they let you draw?"

Blaise sat up, assessed her a moment, and spoke matter-of-factly. "Pencils are deadly weapons. They let me write on a typewriter, though. Hard to kill yourself with a Smith Corona."

Therese knew that, under the shade of that cap, he was watching for a reaction, so she gave him none.

"What are you writing?"

"You really want to know?"

"Yes."

He leaned forward and lifted his brim.

"Do you reallyreallyreallyreallyreally want to know?"

This was the old Blaise, sly smile slanting his words, sparks of mischief in his eyes. Therese felt drawn in, leaned close enough to catch the sourness in his breath.

"Yes, Blaise. Do tell."

"I've been writing a play. A film script, maybe."

"About?"

"Croatian Freedom Fighters."

"Blaise, Jeezus."

"They want to free Croatia so they go around blowing up Serbian mailboxes because they have the Serbian national anthem printed on them. The Serbs take exception to this so they put a price on their heads. The tragedy is that the Croatians don't like the freedom fighters either. They fear freedom, so when a reward is offered, they turn on their own."

"I see." Therese signalled to the waitress while Blaise conjured a massed army from the sugar bowl.

"So, one night after all the mailboxes have been blown up, there's a raid on their headquarters and they get caught and executed. No trial, nothing. Just a firing squad."

"Could we have our bill, please?"

"But one of them gets away. The leader, the Master Freedom Fighter. He holes up in this cathedral and lives in the vaulting for months, just like what's-his-face, the hunchback guy."

"Quasimoto?"

"That's it! He just hangs around up there reading Rousseau in the rafters. The bell ringer is his only friend. He's this little old guy all dressed in burlap. This goes on for months until the bishop finds out and summons a mob. The bell-ringer tries to hold them back, but it's no use. They overpower him and trample him to death. So the Master Freedom Fighter is trapped in the rafters with the mob screaming for his guts. When he refuses to surrender them, storm troops are summoned to scale the pilasters. But just as they reach the top of the columns, he makes his escape."

Blaise's face darkened.

"But how?"

"A trap door, perhaps?" Therese pounced on the bill as soon as the now concerned-looking waitress brought it.

"No, no, no. Too pragmatic." He drummed his fingers and stared out into the hall. His eyes shifted from floor to ceiling, getting wider as they rose. He slammed a fist on the table and sent the cups pirouetting in their saucers.

"That's it! The skylight!"

"Blaise! Take it easy, for God's sake."

"Don't you see? The Albanian air force intervenes. Through the cupola! They skyhook the Master Freedom Fighter to safety in the Macedonian mountains. So, he sits on the highest peak watching albatrosses and waiting for his people to come and build him a clay canoe."

Blaise was on his feet now, arms windmilling.

"A clay canoe? What the hell for?"

"So they can sail to Croatia, of course."

"But Blaise, Macedonia is inland from Croatia. You can't sail from one to the other."

"Sure you can, there's rivers."

"Of course, you're right. You're always right." Therese wasn't sure if this was some kind of joke, or a bona fide psychotic episode, either way it was humiliating and it had been a mistake to meet him like this. She slipped on her coat and scrambled to her feet.

"I've got to go, Blaise. I'm due in court in twenty minutes and there's a movie shoot on Bay Street. They've got the back of Simpson's done up to look like Madison Square Garden."

"Yeah, yeah, of course. Places to go, things to do, missions to fulfill. Madame, take my sword."

He bowed and presented her with the pencil she'd brought him.

"And this," he proffered the pad.

"Don't you want to keep your sketch?"

"No-no-no. It's a token. A wedding present. Our little secret."

Therese crossed the Great Hall with Blaise lagging behind, craning his way through the crowd as he studied the ceiling for more details. She still couldn't accept what Alex and his parents were saying about Blaise; if this was madness, there had to be some method in it.

He followed her all the way out to the taxi rank, across the broad terrace before the station's colonnaded face. The cap looking squarish where he had mauled it in his fingers, the trench coat winging out at his sides, he looked like his father in old army photographs, a cavalryman on leave in some prewar capital. He caught up with her just as the cabbie opened the door for her, snapped his heels together, took up her hand and kissed it.

"Blaise!"

"How about it, Treese. You and me?"

"I don't think so, Blaise. Will you come to the wedding?"

Blaise slipped his arms into his trench coat, drew the belt tight around his waist, and turned up the collar. A gust of wind swept up funnels of dust from the sidewalk, drawing the pigeons with them. Blaise watched them go, lost in thought, or maybe just savouring the moment.

"O-o-o-h, I dunno. Places to go, things to do."

"So what do I tell your brother? What do I tell your parents?"

"Tell 'em ...," he drew up his collar, pulled down his cap brim and took a furtive look up and down Front Street. "Tell 'em I got two hours to find all the Serbian mailboxes in downtown Toronto."

She looked out the back window as the taxi pulled away. There were no exploding mailboxes to be seen, no storm troopers scaling the columns of Union Station, no Albanian aircraft hovering above its cornice work.

Blaise had simply vanished and taken it all with him.

Babayaga

It's a good funeral. The organist plays Chopin's March just so and Father Kulyk sings his "Lord-Be-With-Yous" without a single false note. Old *babcie*, who attend all the funerals at St. Voytek's, jostle to make a show of their piety in the front pews. Babayaga pays no attention to these women. She is not here to make a show.

She kneels at the side altar, with its stumbling Jesus consecrated to the victims of the Hitlerites, and says the prayers she's been commissioned to say by the people of Copernicus Avenue. A woman who has given a dollar for her sick mother in Poland gets a complete cycle of the rosary. A gambler who has given the same for better luck at the race track warrants a lone Hail Mary. The long-haired artist who lives opposite the church has given Babayaga five dollars and asked her to pray for nothing. She suspects he is a communist, so he gets a mere Glory Be. She always prays for Mr. Mienkiewicz, from the Parish Trust, a decade of the rosary once a week. Gratitude for the time he took her to the hospital after she almost froze to death in her telephone booth. He told her not to make a religion out of her disappointments, which still puzzles her.

She takes communion on her knees — with legs stiff as old drain-pipes, this takes some doing — then waddles to the back of the church where she keeps her bundle buggy parked under the choir-loft stairs. Garbage bags of green and orange bloom from its mouth to a height almost twice her own. She tips it gingerly toward herself so that the weight falls square across her shoulders, then she inches her way through the narrow foyer and out onto Copernicus Avenue.

When the funeral cortege emerges, Babayaga is waiting on the sidewalk. Mourners who don't know her stare at the layered clothes that make her wider than she is tall and the straw hat with plastic chrysanthemums woven into the brim. Mourners who do know her give alms to buy prayers for the deceased. Then she moves on for her daily meeting with the Holy Father. Pope John Paul II stands in the little square outside the Parish Trust with his arms outstretched. Babayaga gazes up into the smiling eyes whose pupils the sculptor has cast in the shape of tiny hearts. She kisses the bronze hem of his cassock, then gathers up the cigarette butts on the square and rearranges the flowers the faithful have placed at his feet.

It being the first Thursday of the month, her most important work is at St. Bridget's, the Irish church up past Park Boulevard. To get there, Babayaga must pass the Crippled Civilians store where women line up every Thursday morning when the week's shipment of used goods arrives. Pencilled eyebrows pucker and cashmere berets bob like poppies as the women recoil from her smell. It's the odour of cattle cars and crowded bunkhouses, of a past they have rouged over with husbands and houses and Toni permanents. The women of the Crippled Civilians tell a story about Babayaga and a man who, after she tracked him here through the Red Cross, spent her few dollars on train tickets and headed west with a prostitute he'd met in the Parkdale Tavern. But Babayaga will only say that she is a sinner who is not ashamed to wear the face of God's judgment.

St. Bridget's Church is a Corinthian temple scowling down Copernicus Avenue from atop two long flights of steps. There was a time when Babayaga could climb all the way up on her knees, telling a bead of the rosary at every step. Now it's mortification enough to mount them on her old legs and breathe the heavy air inside the sanctuary. The parish can't pay its heating bills, so dampness nips at Babayaga's knees and ankles. Frescoes of St. Bridget meditating on the passion are streaked with moisture and a whole section of the nave is roped off where masonry has fallen from the ceiling. The red lamp on the altar provides the only light apart from what filters through stained glass dimmed by the unkempt shrubs outside.

Babayaga believes that St. Bridget's has been cursed ever since Monsignor Doyle refused to allow Polish masses. Now the Irish have all moved away and the Monsignor's church is empty except for the children of St. Voytek's parish who still must attend St. Bridget's School even though their families attend the Polish church. On the first Thursday of each month, the children are brought here to confess to the Irish priests and Babayaga comes to show them the proper, Polish way to meet their God.

There is only one class in the church this morning, seven or eight year olds misbehaving in the pews just below the transept as they wait for their turn in the confessional. Their teacher, a nun, prays a few rows back. Babayaga knows this nun with thick glasses and bristles on her chin, a woman who is afraid of everything, who won't make trouble.

She blesses herself with holy water from a seashell held by a glazed angel and starts up the aisle. The children go silent as she reaches the transept, but their giggling resumes as, with great effort, she kneels, beats her breast, and rocks herself until her forehead almost touches the floor.

She knows that the children have named her after the witch Babayaga, and they tell stories of her flying over the neighbourhood in a mortar and pestle. But life has taught her how the Devil puts evil names to good works and she prays that her example will show these children how God's light can burn in strange places.

She takes aside a girl in braids and shows her the proper way to genuflect, head bowed, left hand over the breastbone as the right makes a sign of the cross. The little penitents go stiff in feigned prayer as she wades along the pew behind them.

"What is your name, boy?" she asks a towheaded child.

"Tony Cybulski."

"And what penance did Father give you?"

"Three Our Fathers."

"And what language do you say your prayers in?"

"English."

"If you want God to hear, you must pray in the language of your mother and father."

The boy shakes his head. "I don't know how."

"Then you must repeat." She recites the Lord's Prayer, the boy obediently echoing her in slurred Polish: "*Ojcze nasz, któryś jest w niebie …*"

Babayaga edges her way across the row, scooting behinds off seats and straightening backs. Their bodies harden at her touch. Let them be afraid. Fear is the beginning of real faith.

As she comes to end of the row, a girl emerges from the confessional, walks to the transept with measured steps, makes a perfect genuflection and slips back into her pew. A child from another time in a starched blue dress with puffed sleeves and a Kleenex secured with bobby pins atop her chestnut curls: a little Madonna.

The girl prays in the shadow of the pulpit. There is nothing to correct in the child's attitude. She is a vision. Babayaga eases into the pew for a closer look. It isn't until she's kneeling beside her that she notices the tears dripping from the little Madonna's dark lashes.

"Why do you cry."

"My dog. He ran away."

Babayaga stares as if pondering a stone she had been ordered to uproot without tools. The other children are staring too. So is the nun. At her. It is a test. She must show what a godmother she can be to this girl.

"It is good that you pray for your dog. You must pray to St. Anthony and then maybe even to St. Jude, saint of the lost cause."

The girl cringes and wails as though Babayaga had bared a set of steel teeth. The nun hurries to the confessional door to summon the priest.

"What is your doggy name?"

"Bobby."

"What is he looking like?"

"White with brown and black spots on his back."

"You know what is my name?"

The girl nods, a silver droplet wagging on the end of her nose.

"I have magic. Yes? Not bad magic. Good magic. I use it to find your doggie, but you got to pray to St. Anthony. He give me extra good magic to find it."

The child nods, draws herself up, and prays.

"So you've come back."

Father Leonard, the monsignor's young curate, smiles from the end of the pew. The nun cowers behind him.

"I come for the children," says Babayaga.

"But the children are frightened of you. You tell them the devil will hurt them if they don't do what you say."

"Is true. Devil is waiting. I see him."

"Where do you see him?"

"Queen Street."

The young priest has no answer.

"I do God work," she insists. "I have permission of Father Kulyk."

"Father Kulyk cannot give you permission to do anything at St. Bridget's. Monsignor Doyle is pastor here."

"But you have it Polish children in St. Bridget School. I must help to remember them Polish way."

"Don't they have Polish parents to remind them?"

"Parents only forgetting. I must remember them."

Father Leonard cups her elbow in his hand and escorts her out onto the steps. He helps her all the way down to the nook behind the shrubs where she has hidden her buggy. "You know you are welcome to pray in our church. But you mustn't disturb the children. Here," he says, taking a quarter from a fold in his cassock. "You can pray for me."

Then he gives her his blessing.

Left alone at the foot of the steps, Babayaga feels an impulse to pray, but not for Father Leonard. More like forgiveness. This wanting to be a godmother, to show that she is no witch. It is a selfish thing, a sinful thing. But she has given her word so she will take up her bundles and search in penance for her pride.

Dogs. Dumb brutes without souls. She remembers the strays in Hamburg, roaming in packs after the fire bombings, gnawing at charred bodies, lapping up pools of congealed fat. Dogs think with their guts.

She knows exactly where to begin looking. There is a laneway that traverses the backs of the stores along Copernicus Avenue, where Babayaga competes with rats and strays for the stale loaves and not-yet-rancid scraps consigned to the garbage by shopkeepers.

But it's too early. There are too many delivery trucks in the lane, frightening off the scavengers with their rattling motors. Behind Wong's Fruit and Vegetables, Babayaga encounters her most frequent competitor, a young man with long hair and glasses patched with tape, sorting through a sack of mouldy turnips.

"Have you seen dog?" she asks. "Is little dog. White, brown, black."

The man shakes his head, but offers her a few turnips from the bag. Babayaga accepts them and then turns into the lane that runs behind Westminster Road. Many strays make the laneways their home, people as well as dogs. The weedy aprons between garages are thick with their shit.

"Here, doggy, doggy, doggy," she chants in a voice too low to be heard.

Ramshackle stoops and garages slouch together like Mazovian huts. The empty thoroughfares give easy passage to her and her bundles and she likes looking into the backs of the houses. Unlike the tidy front lawns and porches that project how people want to be seen, the backyards with their sheds, fire escapes, and illegal additions show how people really live. She knows the sheds and thickets where a stray animal might hide. Behind Garland there is a garage where a Portuguese family is secretly fattening a pig. A dog might be drawn there by the smell of the animal's food. She looks in all these places but there is no sign of the dog named Bobby.

She prays to St. Anthony, then to St. Jude. She checks the unlocked garages and narrow alleys where tramps do their business, searching until the sun slips into the treetops and it is time to go home.

The last of the lanes ends in a chain-link fence at the railway corridor that sweeps south toward the lake, a channel of ruins cutting the neighbourhood of Copernicus Avenue off from the city. Babayaga peels back the corroded mesh to allow her and her bundles through.

She eases her buggy up the bank then squats to rest on a switchbox. Without trees, houses, storefronts, and streetcar wires, Babayaga feels held up to the heavens, the same way she felt in Hamburg on mornings after the air raids. She'd crawl from the slit trench that served as the labour camp shelter into air smelling of gasoline and roasted flesh. In the midst of that desolation, the facades of gutted houses fanning out from the labour camp like ceremonial arches, she offered prayers of thanks and felt closer to God than she has ever felt.

She prays to Him now, repents her prideful wish and asks only to perform His will, whatever it may be. Her bundles feel lighter as she sets off, the buggy jouncing over the railway ties.

Walls clouded with the faded signage of Robert Watson Confectionary Ltd. and Reliable Toys give way to fields of rubble that remind her of the lots where she and her labour detail were sent to gather the remains of the incinerated, carrying away whole families in a single basket while the guards pointed at the sky and shouted, "See? See what your friends have done?!" Greenery sprouts along ruined sidings, just like in Hamburg where new trees shot up between the ribs of houses and the fires' heat caused chestnuts and lilacs to bloom twice in a season.

She crosses the trestle at Queen Street and follows a spur into the abandoned yards to her home: the old Sunnyside Station building, uprooted years ago from its place at the foot of Copernicus Avenue, put on a flatcar and rolled onto a disused turntable. Occasionally the railwaymen rotate the turntable to alternate her view between the keep of the Gladstone Hotel and the glass towers of downtown that shimmer like firestorms in the sunset.

The earth around the turntable is littered with chicken bones and other leavings from the meals Babayaga prepares for the tramps whenever they bring something worth cooking. At the station's side door, two planks serve as a ramp for her and her buggy. She enters what was once a cloakroom, walls studded with hooks holding the spades and forks she uses for gardening and self-defence. Then she passes into the ticket hall. Desks and counters show rows of empty sockets where drawers have been extracted and smashed for firewood. Holes in the wall cough up tufts of wire. Brown paper covers the windows and tints everything the colour of old photographs. Shredded railway posters on the walls show ghosts of square-shouldered men with pipes and women in fan-shaped skirts. They smile from comfortable seats and point cameras at mountains and rivers. She remembers seeing these posters on the day she arrived from the boat in Montreal, trying to believe that one day she would be just like those people.

Babayaga drags her buggy over knobs of fallen plaster into the old cafeteria with its serving counter, ice box, and the shell of a griddle and gas range. Smoke escapes through a hole in the roof, coiling up from a hearth made of old bricks and a tin sign for Wilson's Ginger Ale. Scraps of waiting room furniture, draped in scarves and lacework doilies, approximate a parlour setting.

Babayaga doesn't see the two men on the sofa until one stirs himself to rake the embers of the fire with a wrench.

"Heya Babs!" the tramp cackles as he turns and sees her. "We let ourselves in. Had to get Lester here warm."

It's the tramp she calls the filthy one, with face and hands marled in soot and two Red Wing hockey badges pinned and flapping on either side of his toque.

"I was hopin' you could make me a feast."

She turns her attention to the other man, who lies curled under a frayed wool blanket.

"Who owns the Gladstone Hotel?" he asks.

"Don't mind Lester, Babs."

"Does Sir William Pitt own the Gladstone Hotel?"

"He's just dyin'."

"Does Sir William Penn own the Gladstone Hotel?"

She lifts the blanket and looks into the sunken face. Beads of dried blood at the mouth corners, a blackened tongue. His lungs rattle like an old kettle.

"Who owns the Grand Trunk Railroad? Does Sir John Gielgud own the Grand Trunk Railroad?"

"You bring meat?"

The filthy one takes a burlap sack with the faded logo of the Imperial Grain Co.

"Parkdale Grade A number one, Babs."

Babayaga takes the sack from him and feels the weight of it.

"Okay," she says.

"A Thanksgivin'!" The tramp whoops and does a dance that sets the red wings flapping at either side of his head. "Babs is gonna' make a Thanksgivin' feast!"

"Does Franklin Delano Roosevelt own the Gladstone Hotel?"

"You don't got to worry about Lester, Babs. He ain't eaten nothin' or shit nothin' for three days."

"I make him soup."

"No, you don't understand. He don't want soup. I tried him on some Campbell's this mornin'. Right outta the can."

"He will eat my soup."

Babayaga unleashes her bundles, delves down through linens embroidered in the patterns of her village, fringed shawls and scarves printed with garlands of roses and peonies, dresses she never wore, table things, bits of crystal, and picture frames still waiting for children. Halfway down she comes to the knives and cleavers that she carries in velvet-lined cases and lays them out on the table that serves as her cutting board.

She extracts the carcass from the sack. It is a dog, white on its belly, a wedge of pink tongue clamped between its teeth, rimmed in blood. Still breathing. Babayaga feels for the break in its neck and finishes the tramp's clumsy work with an expert twist. Her heart races as she turns it over and looks for the markings. Brown and black, the girl said. But this dog is white as an angel. There are no markings. Babayaga sighs with relief and offers up a quick prayer of thanks.

Such a clever God, she thinks, to correct her pride this way. So that with her soup kettle and a few strokes of her cleaver, she can atone by comforting an old man in his dying hours. His Will be done. She crosses herself and reaches for the skinning knife.

St. David's Day

I

"**M**ove yourself."

The act of rising from bed is carefully plotted: a roll to the left onto his stomach, a slide of the right leg to the floor as he pushes up with his left arm and folds the left leg underneath himself. Thadeus has calculated the stress that each action transfers from his sciatic nerve and arthritic shoulder. His shins are the colour of English sausages, the cracked skin parged with ointment. He has to be careful not to chafe his bloated feet as he slips into the socks he keeps safety pinned to the ankles of his combination underwear. The effort of bending to do so forces him to reach for the puffers on his bedside table. It would be easier to surrender to his throbbing joints, stay home in bed, like the doctor has ordered, and to think as little as possible.

But Thadeus hasn't missed a St. David's Day mass in over fifty years. He is obliged to show he's still in the fight. In sheepskin slippers patched with duct tape, he eases himself down the stairs to a breakfast of shredded wheat and boiled water. It takes longer than it used to for the tubes inside the old radio to warm up, but when it fizzes to life he can't find the weather. Nothing left on the AM band but idiots and sports. He looks out the window. There's his weather. Fog and slush. Perfect.

Freezing mist has kept him under siege for three days. The last stubborn defender of this dingy fortress, he has paced from room to room tallying his unfinished business: wallpaper peeling back to when he and Marlene first shared the house with two other families, closets full of lace-up ski boots and tennis rackets made of wood, the bags upon bags of fabric scraps that Marlene kept bringing home even after she'd forgotten how to quilt. His son Aleksei wants him to move to an apartment in Skaldovia House on Copernicus Avenue.

"Why do you stay in that dungeon?" he asks.

Thadeus finishes dressing in the sun porch, where clothes are draped across furniture in an order that minimizes his need to bend. Herringbone trousers, a green plaid shirt smelling of liniment, blue paisley tie stained with egg yolk. He conceals the ensemble beneath a soldierly suede coat. Crowned with a dapper astrakhan hat, he lowers himself down the porch steps into the slush. Fog bandages the leafless maples and blocks the view of Lake Ontario from the corner of Galway and Copernicus. Headlights turn the streetcar tracks to phosphorous as cars descend the wet pavement from Howard Park Avenue. There are crosswalks a block to either side of St. Voytek's church. But Thadeus knows three people who've been killed on them. So he crosses at the unguarded intersection near Henry's Hardware, where he has always crossed, and enters the church.

It's a thin crowd, though the front pews are filled with the old women who always come to early mass to claim good seats for the funeral mass that follows this one. These *babci* are ageless. Smelling of wet wool in their scarves and galoshes, they could be the same women who jostled for the best places when St. Voytek's opened its doors forty years ago.

"Glory being on the Father, son in the Holy Ghost, Amen."

The priest is a kid fresh from Poland; he's been given the early mass to practise his English. It's a good thing that Thadeus hasn't brought his hearing aid to church. When he finally makes arrangements for himself at G.W. Patterson's funeral home, he will state explicitly that this stammering youngster is not to say his funeral mass. And the organist: anything but that miserable funeral march of Chopin's. The organ drones in his failing ears, a reminder of Merlin engines and his purpose here. He slips a faded mass card from his missal and begins his annual string of prayers for the souls of Youzek, Bugajski, Prus, Kadarek, Darwinski, and Królik. His cataracts make it easy to project their faces into the cluster of saints in the stained glass: Youzek studying the heavens, Kadarek winking from under his fringe of dark curls, the others frowning as if they were impatient for Thadeus to join them.

St. David seems a little fed up with him, too. The mitred saint on the mass card has a face that only a mad Welshman could love: sallow, weathered as the rock he stands on. An unfortunate dove is nailed to his shoulder. He's a stern patron, this saint who lived on bread crusts and recited scripture while immersed to the neck in freezing water. No wonder his own monks tried to poison him.

II

HEAVEN AND HELL — THE war turned everything upside down. In those days hell was in the heavens: a searchlit sky choked with shrapnel and men's guts. Heaven was down below, a debriefing shed with a stove to warm your frozen hands, Lucky Strikes, and a shot of His Majesty's rum to settle your nerves. The line that separated the two straddled the towers of Lincoln Minster.

In their circuits in and out of Faldingworth, Thadeus always plotted a course above the cathedral overlooking the Lincolnshire plain. On the way out, its conical spires and scaly fold of roof were reminders to cross yourself because the odds were two-to-one you wouldn't be coming back. On the way in, especially on a moonlit night, the Minster's limestone facade shone up at them like the pearly gates.

"*0200 hrs. March 1, 1945. N. 53°, 20'. W. 27'. Position: Lincoln.*"

Thadeus wrote the final entry for their fourteenth operation in his navigator's log then drew back the curtain of his cabin for his ritual good luck glance at the ground. That particular morning, the towers and buttresses appeared to levitate toward them on a silk cushion as tendrils of ground fog congealed at the foot of the cathedral hill. "Good thing we're not late," Youzek, their skipper, muttered into his headphones. "Another half hour and we'd be fogged in." Then he banked M Mother into its final approach. Two-seven-zero starboard. After fourteen ops, Youzek knew the heading by heart.

Thadeus folded his charts, gathered up his slide rule, protractors, squares, compasses, and pencils, and stowed them in crisp leather satchels under his table. The crew teased him about his neatness, same way they teased him about his age, nicknamed him "Daddy" Mienkiewicz because he was almost thirty.

Thadeus buckled himself into his crash seat on the bulkhead which gave him a clear view through the windscreen over Youzek's shoulder. Blue exhaust flames of two Lancasters were visible on the circuit ahead of them, the lead plane rounding to starboard. Youzek followed and the nose dipped to show the purple lights of the flare path just visible in the mist.

Then the night turned orange and a shock wave bucked him hard forward against his harness. A shower of debris peppered M Mother's skin and something big swept over the canopy a few feet from their heads.

"*Jezus Maria!*"

"Bandits!"

Two jets of yellow tracer burst from the night fighter's wing roots as it shot past them. The sky went orange again, then black as they passed through a cloud stinking of burnt oil. Everyone was shouting. Prus, Królik, and Darwinski were back in their turrets, their guns chattering wildly into the dark, cutting the oily stench with the sharp smell of cordite. Bugajski, the flight engineer, lunged at the throttles while Youzek strained back on the control column. The engines howled as M Mother pulled into an agonized climb.

The WAAF controller in Faldingworth tower broke through in a voice as close to panic as an Englishwoman would allow herself. "Domino Control to all incoming aircraft. Abort your approaches and scramble. We repeat, abort your approaches and scramble."

M Mother corkscrewed upwards toward a sheet of stratus advancing from the northwest. Once the plane was flying straight and level in the cloud cover, Thadeus unbuckled and returned to his table to plot a holding pattern. His hands shook as he reattached his instruments to their elastic tethers. Two shocks, fore and aft: the planes in front and behind them. M Mother had been spared as Jerry paused between bursts. He turned on the Gee set mounted on the bulkhead to his left. Two orange vectors, beacons from the south of England, intersected at their position. Thadeus traced them onto his map, then drew a plot west of the River Trent between Leeds and Doncaster, far enough inland to make the intruders think twice about pursuing.

"Port one five zero, skipper."

There was more than enough fuel to keep them circling for a few minutes until the all-clear came. Thadeus switched off his lamp and stepped up behind the pilot's seat. The sky was becoming a complicated place. Thick cumulus puffed down from the north while the fog below turned brownish yellow where it merged with the smoke of the industrial Midlands. Three separate fronts of heavy weather converging at the point where the blacked-out mass of Sheffield stained the English countryside.

"Weather's really closing in," said Youzek. "They'd better bring us down soon."

Fifteen minutes since the order to abort. He looked back around the bulkhead at Jan Kadarek, the radio operator, huddled at his set, gauntlets off, tossing a pair of dice alongside his notepad on the square tabletop. The receiver's red light was on, the voice frequency to Faldingworth open. Another five minutes. No signal. Thadeus extended the vector on his map a quarter inch.

"Youzek, that weather's moving fast. We should contact base."

"King's regulations, Daddy," Kadarek piped in. "When Jerry's about, we speak only when we're spoken to."

"Daddy's right, Jasiu," the pilot countered. "We've been up here long enough."

Kadarek threw the toggle on the transmitter. "All yours, Skipper."

"Domino Control. This is M Mother. Do you read?"

The WAAF's voice came back in a barrage of interference. "This is Domino. We read you, M Mother."

"Request permission to land, Domino."

"Negative, M Mother. We are fogged in. All bases in this sector now report zero visibility."

The big pilot surveyed the racing clouds and shook his head. "Young lady," he purred, "why do you wait so long with this happy news?"

"We signalled all aircraft to divert ten minutes ago. You did not acknowledge. Thought we'd lost you."

Stunned silence where Youzek's response should have been.

"Recommend you bear southwest and ..." The woman's voice crackled apart in the static. Then the signal disappeared altogether.

III

THADEUS CAN'T BEAR THE thought of another day's confinement. "Move yourself," he thinks. "To the park."

High Park has been his fixed star, his Polaris. He can walk its trails and recognize the hollows where he and the other boys from the navigational school at Malton made love to the girls they'd seduced to the strains of Bert Niosi, "Canada's King of Swing," at the Palais Royale. He can rest on the same benches where he courted Marlene after the war, watch himself totter on skates across the frozen duck pond as his boys cut circles around him, search again for Blaise, his youngest, who is still eight years old and waiting to be found in a culvert under Bloor Street. This is where he comes to be all the things he's ever been, to fool himself that it's all far from over.

But today the park refuses to co-operate. The old playing field is an arcade of cherry trees. Mature trees. Where did they find time to grow? And who scribbled over the boys' tobogganing slopes with dogwood?

The duck pond was once precisely landscaped with miniature stone temples and stocked with goldfish as a gift from the city of Osaka. Now bulrushes clog the shore and the goldfish have bloated and blackened into mud-sucking carp. They've made a swamp of the place. "Natural regeneration," say the signs along the shore. Thadeus tries to read the explanations, but his English fails him just as it failed him during Aleksei's last visit, when he started jabbering at the boy in Polish, forgetting that his sons can't speak a word. It's like Marlene told him before she started slipping away: "The older you get, the more Polish you become." Perhaps he's regenerating too, just like those goldfish.

The tubular iron spaceships and dinosaurs of the playground have vaporized. In their place stands a dull-looking wooden fort. The snack bar has been torn from its place, leaving a socket of sand-coloured dirt, the same colour as the earth piled by Marlene's grave on the day of her funeral. The gravediggers couldn't keep the sides from collapsing as they dug. Had to leave her by the road in that vault the funeral directors at Patterson's had talked Aleksei into buying. No one's going to put him in a cement box. He'll make sure, go to Pattersons, make those arrangements. Soon.

IV

"*0237 hrs. N. 53°, 37'. W. 001°, 12'. Position: W. of Doncaster.*"

"Kadarek, you and that slut of a radio again!" It was Królik, his voice raw with the hours of watching in the frigid rear turret.

"Whatsamatter, Rabbit," Johnny sang back in his Americanized English. "Out of carrots?"

Sharp-tongued, quick with his fists when he'd had a few, Królik had had it in for Kadarek ever since a little disagreement at the Saracen's Head over a farm girl from Louth. They all called him "Rabbit" because that's what his name meant in Polish, but Kadarek like to rub it in by hanging carrots in his turret before each operation, saying it was because they were good for the eyes.

"That radio's been acting up for weeks. You should have been fucking with it instead of the girls at the Saracen's."

"Shut up, Rabbit," Thadeus cut in.

"Yessirree, Daddy! Wouldn't want to upset your golden boy."

The oldest and the youngest men in the squadron, Thadeus and Johnny Kadarek worked the pubs in Lincoln as a team. Johnny drew the girls to their table with his John Garfield good looks and the chocolate, nylons, cigarettes, and perfume he kept on hand thanks to the nimble fingers he'd developed as a pickpocket in Siberia. Once Johnny had them "in the tent," as his American friends said, Thadeus mesmerized them with his cavalryman's charm. Nothing to it, really: English girls were defenceless against men who actually paid attention to them. Thadeus's attachment to Kadarek had a more practical foundation than womanizing. After watching the young wireless operator disassemble and reassemble a transmitter blind-folded at the OTU — the Operational Training Unit — in Shrewsbury, Thadeus knew those quick hands could come in handy in the air.

Kadarek possessed one other thing that Thadeus coveted: an easy relationship with death. In the dispersal hut before their first operation, as Thadeus struggled to manage the contents of his stomach, Johnny conjured a Lucky from his sleeve, lit it and passed it to him with a steady hand. "Come on, Daddy," he drawled. "Don't be chicken." Having watched his parents die of cholera and his brothers being beaten to death for stealing food, Johnny bought lightly into the belief that they had been dead men the minute they pinned on their wings. Now, with disaster teasing the Lancaster's big round wingtips, Johnny Kadarek sat on the other side of the bulkhead, indifferent to all prospects of a future and humming Glen Miller tunes over the intercom as he checked his radio, circuit by circuit.

The plane began to shudder

"Turbulence," Youzek called. "Everybody buckle in. Daddy, I need a course."

Thadeus broke the seals on his maps for Wales and the southwest. "What's the fuel situation, Boog?"

"Maybe two hundred gallons including the reserve tanks."

Enough to get them to the sea where Coastal Command would have bases with runways big enough for them.

"It's either Wales or Devon, then." The prevailing winds were southwesterlies. Not good. All they could do was pray that a local system would cough up a good tailwind. Thadeus confirmed their position on the Gee. Forty miles due east of Manchester. Then he pencilled a vector southwards on his map. At Bristol, they could veer either toward Wales or the south coast depending on the winds, the weather, and, above all, the radio.

"Steer two four zero, skipper." The Lancaster swung about and pitched as the wind hit it broadside. Thadeus noted their course and position, his letters blurring with the vibrations. It was two forty-five. He had to find somewhere to land by four a.m.

Thadeus was reaching up to switch off the Gee set when his stomach leapt to his mouth. His slide rule squares and protractors shot up from the desk and wavered on the ends of their tethers. Then he heard his spine crunch as thirty-seven thousand pounds of aircraft plunged one hundred feet straight down and stopped with a sickening crack.

"What in the plague's name ..."

"Wind shear, skipper!"

"*Jezus* ..."

"FIRE!"

Sparks showered down from the racks over his table and his office filled with smoke that tasted of metal. Thadeus lunged to protect his charts. Boog was on top of him with a fire extinguisher, coating the compartment with bluish retardant which choked him more than the smoke. When it cleared they stared in disbelief at the Gee set straining away from its fitters on scorched cables.

"Crew call in."

"Tail gunner OK."

"Bomb aimer OK."

"Mid Upper Gunner OK."

"Wireless report."

Panic whited out the searing pain in his lower back. Without Gee and without radio they were deeply, deeply in the shit.

"Wireless, report!" The aircraft still jouncing in the turbulence, pain stabbing down his legs and into his fingertips at each bounce, he crept round the bulkhead and shone his torch into the wireless compartment. Kadarek knelt in a litter of tools, coils, clips, and shattered glass, his movie star's jawline speckled with blood where splinters from an exploding vacuum tube had scored the left side of his face. He wore an expression of blank, animal terror.

"The crystals. I can't find the spare crystals."

Behind him, the transmitter dangled from the table by its connections, knots of coloured wire spilling from its open back and the glass filament essential for tuning the radio shattered in its housing. Thadeus spotted the case of spares under some debris at the foot of the flare chute. Quaking with the pain, he stooped to retrieve it then pressed it into the Johnny's arms. "Act as if none of it matters," he told himself, "believe that none of it matters. We're already dead men, so what can possibly happen?"

"Here they are. Now. Jasiu. Fix that radio. It's a piece of pudding, yes?"

The boy's breath steadied and his eyes twinkled.

"Cake, Daddy. It's a piece of cake."

V

UP DEER PEN ROAD, his old friends wait in chain-link pens. Yaks, Highland Cattle, Longhorn Sheep, hides flecked with wood chips, shanks matted with frozen mud. They could be the same creatures that Blaise and Aleksei fed with crusts when they were small, laughing as the Virginia Deer nibbled at their pockets and licked their palms. The smell of hay and droppings and the shaggy patient hulls of animals, these had been the sights and smells of his own childhood. Deer Pen Road was the closest he could get the boys to that vanished world. After Marlene went into the home, he came here with Ela, the niece who came from Poland to stay with him for a few months. Ela had been a girl of six when the war began and was old enough to remember the stables and barnyards of the family's settlement in Polesie. But she burst into tears at the sight of the animals sulking in their overcrowded pens.

He stayed away after that, for a while, but now it's a comfort to see the buffalo and the reindeer standing exactly where he had left them. Today, Thadeus is their only visitor and the animals come right to the fence for handouts. He feels uncomfortable, as if he were the exotic specimen, not them. Something dumb and lugubrious in the stare of the bison, like those crazy nuts who come in off the streets at Patterson's to gaze into the open caskets of strangers. He'll leave instructions to keep his casket closed.

Beyond the animal pens, the road turns up to the ridge that overlooks Grenadier Pond. Its surface is a tongue of sheer ice cratered with green smears of goose shit. Thadeus picks his way up the slope until, halfway up, he finds himself unable to move on the slippery surface. His feet lose purchase. Knees shake in the effort to stay erect and his sciatic nerve sparks against the old back injury. Perhaps this is what's been waiting for him all these years: old man visits park against doctor's orders, old man gets stuck on ice, struggles, falls, breaks hip, freezes to death before anyone finds him. It seems there are only stupid ways to die, usually involving bad weather. He could just sit down and let winter do the rest. Exposure. Not such a bad way to go. Like falling asleep. That's how they used to describe the likely outcome of ditching in the sea.

Give in. Thadeus has seen people do it. A man in his escape party through the Carpathians, a writer from Lwów who squatted in the snow and refused to get up. They left him there to freeze, and the man's face has haunted him ever since — the face of surrender. He saw it one other time during the war, when he was still in the army, his unit guarding a beach in Scotland. The kid from Grodno, a private in his platoon, who came to his tent and announced he was returning to Poland. Thadeus thought it was a joke the others had put the kid up to, so he laughed and sent him packing. That afternoon the kid walked into the sea in full kit. The tide took him out and he washed up at Montrose two days later. Nowadays he sees defeat in the faces of friends who survived everything — battle, torture, imprisonment — only to let themselves rot in seniors' apartments. God sets these people in front of you for a reason — to remind you that, whatever happens, you've got to move yourself.

"Don't be chicken," he mutters, feet kneading the insoles of his boots, looking for a hold on the ice. Left foot: heel, toe. Right foot: heel, toe. Goose shit collects on his toe caps as he edges toward the glacier's edge. Tufts of dead grass poke through ice at the side of the road. Thadeus gets close enough to grab one, pulls himself within reach of another and then another until he's at the top of the bank, sucking greedily at his puffer. Easier not to be a chicken, he thinks, when you had no idea how much there was to live for.

VI

"*0305 hrs. N. 52º, 15'. W. 002º. Position: Birmingham.*"

Dead reckoning. All guesswork now. He watched the compass for the slightest change of heading, studied the airspeed for any variation. He held himself alert to any buffeting that might signal a change in the wind and kept his slide rule in constant motion as he calculated and recalculated each course correction. Every seven minutes he traced over another centimetre of his vector in red pencil. Thadeus used the pain in his back as a goad to keep himself alert. The flight became a litany of notes and observations as he made log entries in his carefully squared handwriting. He recorded everything that the pilot and flight engineer did to save fuel, their terse exchanges about revolutions, oil pressures, and fuel mixtures. He would tuck the book into his flak suit, so that after they scraped him out of the wreckage in a farmer's field, they would learn how the crew of M Mother had worked like soldiers right to the end, and no stuffed shirt at the Air Ministry could write them off as a pack of crazy Poles who'd got lost in the fog.

South of Birmingham, God granted them a tailwind. Youzek sat fused to his controls, hand gripping the trim wheel, feet working the rudder bar, keeping the Lancaster absolutely straight and level to minimize drag, a hellish way to fly after seven hours in the air.

"Be careful who you take," his Canadian instructor had said, "And never sign on with a pilot until you've shaken his hand."

At Shrewsbury, Youzek didn't give out handshakes to just anyone. While the younger trainees at Shrewsbury spent evenings at the pub with pilots who were sharp at cards, Thadeus followed the solitary Silesian around the machine shops and travelled with him out to Lincolnshire on their leaves to get an advance look at the new Lancasters. He learned how Youzek had disobeyed French orders to surrender in 1940, flown his plane to Algeria, then crossed the desert to join the British. He had to lend the man an instruction manual in order to get a handshake as thanks. When he felt the sureness of that grip, he knew he had his pilot.   .

Youzek's sure hands had already saved them once, when ice glazed over M Mother's wings on a trip to Holland. That had been their first visit to the next world's waiting room. Now the door to that room was open again.

A bang and a cough from the port inner engine.

"They're missing!" called Darwinski from his vantage point in the upper turret.

"Keep your trousers on," Bugajski answered as he made some adjustments to the fuel cocks.

Bugajski, they called him Boog, after the Polish word for God, because of his divine ability to sense every part of the aircraft as he fussed over its pumps and switches. Bugajski was a most benevolent God, always fixing up old cars and motorbikes for his mates, or rigging illegal heaters in the barracks when the dank English weather became more than the Poles could bear. When the call went up for more volunteers for aircrew, his fellow mechanics had dubbed him "Village Idiot" for signing on after three years of scraping guts out of shattered cockpits.

The coastal command stations in Devon were still thirty minutes away. They would arrive in the area with minutes to spare. But without radio or a break in the weather, how would they find a base? The aircraft was enveloped in a mantle of yellow fog. No chance of a visual fix on the ground. To climb above the weather for a star shot would be a reckless waste of fuel.

New winds began to buffet them and the Merlin engines snarled in an effort to stay on course.

"Wind's shifting, Daddy. We need to keep this tailwind. What happens if we bear west?"

"Wales. There are bases that could take us in Pembrokeshire."

"Give us the heading."

"Hey," cried Prus, the bomb aimer, "aren't there mountains in Wales?"

"Highest peaks in Britain. Make a barge pole out of something, Prus. Your job is to keep us off the rocks."

The joke was aimed at Prus's prewar occupation as a boatman in the Carpathians. He was right to be nervous. The Welsh mountainsides were studded with wrecks of aircraft that had lost their way in fogs. At the moment, they had enough altitude to get over them. What worried Thadeus was the sea. Instinct told him the new winds were pushing them northwest, but how far and how fast? When would he know they had crossed the coast? He flicked the toggle on his H2S radar set. The new sets were supposed to give navigators an impression of the ground, even through cloud cover, but they were notoriously unreliable. The green haze on the screen could have been anything. They banked west and M Mother bobbed on masses of sea air pushing up over the invisible hills below.

"Jasiu, what's with that radio?"

"Don't worry, skipper. I'm building us a new one!"

Three-forty. At Faldingworth, they would have been posted missing by now. The last crews through debrief were sitting down to their powdered eggs and meatless sausages and trying not to look at the empty places set for the crew of M Mother.

They had known the odds when they signed up for Bomber Command, but Thadeus had thought the end would come in a burst of flame over Stuttgart or Bremen. If such a death gave you any time to think, he had expected to feel that the sacrifice had been worth it.

"So boys, if we die, I think we should all agree on who we're dying for ..."

"Rabbit ..."

"Churchill, Roosevelt, or Stalin? What's your choice?"

"I think you should kiss my ass, Rabbit."

On every flight, Thadeus had carried a letter from his sister in his battledress pocket, the letter telling him that his father, his brothers, and their wives and children had died in the massacre at Baranica. He carried the letter on every flight to keep his thoughts clear as M Mother rained fire on Hamburg and Dresden.

"For me, Churchill's a little too fat. Roosevelt's too sick."

"You're the one who's sick, Rabbit."

No one had had a clearer idea of what they were fighting for. In Poland, they had been the first to stand up to Hitler. In Britain they signed up for the Free Polish Forces younger and served longer than the British, or the Americans, or the Canadians. Darwinski had been shot down over Warsaw then walked across Europe on a broken leg to fight on, while the French sat behind the Maginot Line and the British dropped leaflets. Królik had crossed the Baltic in a rowboat. Thadeus had crossed the Carpathians on foot with the NKVD and the Gestapo two steps behind. Thousands, like Kadarek, had clawed their way out of the Gulag. From the Battle of Britain to Monte Cassino, to Falaise, to Arnheim, they took the toughest assignments — for the sake of honour, because honour was all they had left.

"I say we vote for Papa Joe. At least with Stalin, we all know what we're getting into."

"You forget, Rabbit, we're not allowed to vote on anything."

"Yeah. Churchill and Roosevelt make the decisions for us."

Two weeks earlier the squadron had gathered in the mess and listened in stunned silence to the terms the leaders of the Grand Alliance had agreed to at Yalta. Parents, wives, children, homes, farms, and cities — Roosevelt and Churchill had given the lot to Stalin. Fearing a mutiny, the British confiscated Polish officers' side-arms at one base. At another, Poles had been restricted to barracks.

"They sold us out," someone protested at that day's pre-op briefing. "So why should we go?" No one stayed behind that night, and three planes were lost in their attack on a target blocking the Russian advance.

Stalin's propagandists were hard at work in Britain. At the OTU in Shrewsbury, British communists painted the perimeter wall with slogans calling the Poles warmongers and worse. Some Polish airmen had started borrowing Czech uniforms to go into London.

"Rabbit, what are you going to do when this is over?" asked Bugajski, the optimist.

"Me, I'm going to work the black market with Kadarek, until I get so rich I can hire a fine English butler and call him a traitor to his face every day at tea time."

"I will go home," said Darwinski. "To Poland!"

"*Idiota!*" Królik scoffed. "Stalin's already locking up anyone who fought in the uprising. What do you think he'll do to us?"

They flew on, but something had changed. Heaven and hell. Black and white. Until Yalta, the distinctions had been intoxicatingly clear. Now there were days when everything seemed as muddled as the haze on Thadeus's radar screen. A new campaign had opened inside each man's head: the battle to make it all mean something.

"Shut up, the lot of you." Youzek's voice, edged with fatigue, hacked into the conversation. "No one's dying for anyone tonight. Not Stalin, not Churchill, not the Holy Mother herself. I didn't drag my ass to this soggy island to run out of petrol in the fog. So button your mouths and do your jobs. Kadarek!"

"Okay, skipper. I'm trying again."

No one breathed as Kadarek began his transmission, hailing the RAF's distress centre.

"Darky, Darky. This is M Mother."

Nothing.

"Darky, where are you hiding, you poxy bastard?"

"Shut up, Rabbit."

"It's no good, skipper. There's no signal."

"Sure you've thought of everything?"

"Everything, skipper."

"Then try something you haven't thought of."

Thadeus unbuckled and, defying the fire in his lower back and legs, pulled himself out of his seat for a look around the bulkhead. Kadarek sat ashen-faced in the light of his torch, lips working feebly against engines' roar. Thadeus tried to force his thoughts through the pain to a place where he could find words to buck the kid up. Nothing. Then a figure tumbled out of the darkened catwalk. Królik pulled himself upright in his heavy tail gunner's togs and glared at his archrivals.

"Oi, shit-for-brains. There's thirty miles of wire in this plane. Show me where to look. Let's fix this thing."

As Johnny and Rabbit began inspecting the pipes that held the plane's wiring, Thadeus crumpled back into his seat, folded his hands over his charts, and prayed. "Our Father," he said. "I know we have said we are ready to die, but so many have died already. Send us a saint. Any saint. Maybe someone who's not so popular, who could use our prayers. Send a saint to help us and I will honour that saint in everything I do."

"Daddy, where the hell are we? Land or sea?"

Thadeus flicked on the H2S. The screen registered a perfect blank, possibly water, possibly nothing at all. He looked at his map and checked his watch. Three fifty-six. They were minutes from the point at which their fuel should run out. He penciled another centimetre onto their course vector. "My guess is we're over the Irish Sea, Cardigan Bay, maybe seventy miles south of Anglesey."

"Let's see if you're right."

Youzek put the nose down and Thadeus felt his bowels clench as the plane descended through the clouds.

VII

THE BENCH IS EXACTLY where he wanted it, on the ridge above Grenadier Pond and the formal gardens. Thadeus dusts the snow from the seat and uses his keys to scrape ice from the brass plaque that reads, "In Memory of Marlene Mienkiewicz, who loved this place." Today, the view is a child's pencil sketch, half-erased in the fog, rock gardens, stands of yew and boxwood reduced to smudges and linked by helixes of snow fence.

They courted here in the summer of '51, Sunnyside amusement park still whirling and clattering down by the lake and survivor's euphoria running like amphetamine in his veins. He turned aside the Polish girls the community had urged toward him and chose a Canadian woman. They were both in their thirties — old, in those days, to be starting at anything. But the world he had known in Polesie had been swept away. His children would be Canadians. Marlene and the boys were his new beginning and, in the beginning, Thadeus thought that was all his new patron saint could expect of him.

It wasn't easy. He studied accounting at night and worked at the Eaton's warehouse by day. He and Marlene bought the house on Galway, rented out rooms to pay the mortgage. Eventually, he thought, he would move their new family to Mississauga, buy a station wagon, maybe even learn to like hockey.

But his patron saint hadn't finished with him. The army of Free Poland had a new beachhead, on the shore of Lake Ontario. Instead of guns and planes, they needed capital to start businesses and buy homes. No Canadian bank would lend to them, so Father Kuron set up the Parish Trust and asked Thadeus to head the loan committee. He took the job, at half the salary he'd finally been offered by the Dominion Life Assurance Company after he finished his course.

The salary increased over the years, but he and Marlene never left

Copernicus Avenue. There would be no station wagon for him, no house with a driveway. He stayed on the front line, equipping carpenters, electricians, mechanics, and shopkeepers with the means to win back their dignity, a navigator charting courses for new lives. This was what he had been spared for. This was the will of the pale saint that God had conjured out of the fog.

Interventions in family disputes, intercessions with the Polish consulate, lobbying members of Parliament and city councillors: does his patron have all that marked down in his ledger? What about the Polish Combatants' Association, the Legion, the Air Force Association? What about the weekend meetings, the evening committee work, parcels to Poland, fundraising for monuments and medicines? Thadeus wants to know how his account stands. Sum or difference? Credit or debit?

And how does his saint reckon the impact of this war without end on his family? Does he have a column in his book for collateral damage? His sons have grown into strangers. Aleksei, MBA, CA, has done all the right things and acts as if he resents having been made to do them. Then Blaise, the arteeste, forty years old, still living like he's fourteen.

"What do you know about family?" Marlene asked him once, during one of their arguments about the boys. Hard to reconcile an upbringing in the marshes with a world of computers and television and nuclear families. Nothing had ever quite measured up, not in his sons, not in himself.

He had done his duty. He had provided, for the boys, and then for Marlene through the years it took her to fade away, word by word, trait by trait, oblivious to his daily visits at the home, through the hours it took to dress her and wedge a little food between her lips. Until there was nowhere left to move himself to except this bench, nothing to do except appeal to his saint for final orders.

VIII

BUGAJSKI CALLED OUT THE altitude. "Seven thousand feet ... Six thousand ... Forty-five hundred ... Three thousand ..."

"Have that barge pole ready, Prus," said Youzek. "Everybody watch for hills."

Under two thousand feet the possibility of meeting with a peak or cliff face was very real. Thadeus's headphones throbbed with the rapid breathing of the others.

"One thousand feet ... Five hundred."

Darwinski, who decorated his turret with mass cards, was softly praying.

"Two hundred feet!"

Still nothing.

"One hundred feet —"

"Water! There! Pull up! For Christ's sake, pull up!" It was Prus down in the nose. Thadeus strained for a look through the windscreen as a grey roller lifted a foamy paw toward them. Youzek hauled the plane up into the mist and levelled off at five hundred feet.

"Well, we know we're over water," he said. "You were right, Daddy. Congratulations."

Thadeus steadied himself as another bolt of pain sliced at his hamstrings. Then he checked their heading and made an entry in his log.

"*0407 hrs. N. 53°, 10'. W. 005°, 10'. Position: WNW. of Cardigan (?).*"

The Lancaster had to be running on fumes.

"All I know for sure is we're heading out to sea, Youzek. We don't want to go any farther."

"What does the coast look like?"

Thadeus studied his map, tallying the contour lines tightly

clustered at the Welsh coastline. Did they head for land and risk hitting a mountain before they could bail out, or did they stay over water and face the prospect of ditching? "If we're where I think we are, the hills come right to the shore and you'd need at least eighteen hundred feet to get over them."

"Me," Prus offered. "I feel like a swim."

"Moron! In that sea we'd be dead in five minutes."

"And what? You'd rather die with Mount Snowdon up your arse?"

"No one's dying anywhere," Youzek snapped. "We can't waste fuel in a climb. We'll stay over water and wait for developments."

"Developments. Ha! That'd be you, Kadarek."

"I'm working on it!"

The wireless operator shimmied down the catwalk over the bomb bay, framed by Królik's torch as he picked through the wires he'd unleashed from their piping.

On the flight deck, Thadeus could see how much harder Youzek and Bugajski had to lean into the controls in the heavier winds. The flight engineer gripped the throttles and trim wheel while straining to watch his gauges, giving Youzek two hands to work the column as if he was welded to it. The strain was audible in the pilot's voice as he ordered Prus and Darwinski to lighten their load. A blast of cold salty air shot up through the cabin as Prus opened the nose hatch and drew his twin Brownings out of the forward turret. Darwinski did the same at the rear door. The guns were followed by ammo boxes, flares, oxygen bottles, first aid equipment, Prus's bombsight, and the armour plate on the back of Youzek's seat.

"Skipper, I think I've found something." It was Kadarek who had traced the wiring halfway down the plane. Looks like we took some shrapnel. It stripped some wires."

"Fix them."

At the rear of the plane, Darwinski demolished the Elsan toilet, jettisoned its remnants, then tossed out the axe he'd been using. Thadeus remembered the formula they'd been taught at OTU: a pound of weight is a foot of altitude, a foot of altitude is a gallon saved, a gallon saved is another minute in the air. He recited it like a novena, until Johnny Kadarek's voice broke through.

"Darky, Darky. This is M Mother. Do you read?"

The pounding of the engines ceased registering as the crew listened into the static for a response.

"M Mother. This is Darky. We've been expecting your call."

The plummy tones of the controller were lost under the men's howl of relief.

"Shut up. Shut up all of you." Youzek's voice cracked then ironed itself smooth for his answer. "Darky, this is M Mother. Our situation is critical. Request direction to nearest available landing ground."

"That will take some doing M Mother. All sectors report zero visibility."

"I repeat. Our fuel situation is critical. We have only minutes left."

"Roger, M Mother. Please stand by."

Someone cursed the unflappable English.

"Pembroke sector reports some local clearing, M Mother. Navigator mark your position. Five degrees, west longitude by fifty-two degrees, two minutes north latitude." Thadeus made a fist to stop his fingers from trembling, then took up his pencil. Incredible. Two hours of blind flight and they were only a few miles south of the position he'd plotted. "We recommend you bear starboard three zero. You'll be hearing from your hosts momentarily."

The plane banked right as Thadeus sketched in the new heading. They would just graze the tip of the Pembroke peninsula, where his map showed a dozen bases within a few miles of one another.

"Roger your instructions, Darky. We are proceeding as directed."

"Land!" Darwinski cried. "Straight ahead."

The fog had lifted just enough to show a charcoal smudge separating the slate sea from clouds that had begun to turn purple as dawn approached. "It isn't home," said Prus. "But I'll take it."

"I'll marry it!" cried Królik. "I'll give it children!"

Britain answered his proposal with the voice of a young Welshwoman. "M Mother, this is Blackthorn control. Roger your clearance for landing. Continue on your present heading. We advise caution on approach, conditions variable, ceiling three hundred feet with intermittent fog. Your range is thirty miles north-northwest."

The WAAF began a long list of questions. Damage? Wounded? Payload status? Fuel levels? Youziu spat back his answers as if all fifteen tons of the aircraft were resting on his shoulders. Thadeus offered a prayer to their new patron saint, whichever one it might be. Nothing ever felt as clear to him as this white-hot desire to live.

The dark brow of the coastline furled and unfurled between shifting swatches of mist until they could distinguish cliffs. Bugajski revved them up to a keening pitch that drew them up over the familiar patchwork of the British countryside.

"M Mother, we have you tracking straight on five miles north-northeast. Ceiling at base is two hundred feet and dropping. Visibility two hundred yards and closing."

"We should see them by now. Where are their lights?"

The clouds brushed the canopy and reduced details on the ground to dark swatches.

"M Mother. We have local fog re-entering the area. Visibility fifty yards and closing. Proceed vector oh-nine-five to RAF Haverfordwest."

"They're diverting us!" Thadeus looked at his charts, lines blurring as cold sweat poured into his eyes. "That's another fourteen miles, Youzek."

"We'll never make it," said Bugajski.

Królik, Prus, and Darwinski rained more oaths on the English, on Churchill, and the Welsh WAAF.

"Enough!" Youzek shouted. "Enough, all of you! Keep your heads." Then he addressed the tower with perfect English calm.

"This is M Mother. Our fuel gauges read nil. Request clearance to land."

Another pause as the WAAF referred to silent superiors. "Negative your request, M Mother. Ceiling and visibility are below limits."

"Negative your refusal," the pilot shot back. "We are declaring an emergency. I repeat, we are declaring an emergency and are preparing for a crash landing."

Switching back to the intercom, Youzek called to Kadarek, "Jasiu, I want no more words with these Limeys. You talk from now on. Everyone else take your crash positions. If they won't help us, we'll go in on our belly."

A church spire shot past the port wingtip. "*Jezus!* That was close."

Thadeus made one last plot check.

"The airfield should be about a mile straight on."

Then he stuffed his instruments into their cases, stowed them and curled into his crash position. They were barely sixty feet from the ground, the canopy whited over, as if the Lancaster was boring through a bale of dirty silk. An engine sputtered, then fell back into synch.

"Two more minutes, Boog. Keep them turning." Youzek growled between grit teeth. "Where the hell is it?"

Then a cry from Prus, keeping watch until the last minute in the nose blister.

"Skipper, look, look!"

It was the most unearthly sight Thadeus had ever seen; a silver platform appeared in the air ahead of them, searchlights aimed down the length of a runway. A series of orange balls blossomed alongside it: flashpots full of burning petrol to burn off the fog.

"M Mother this is Dogwood control. You have our permission to land. Range four hundred yards and closing. Good luck skipper. Good luck, good luck ..."

They heard the scraping of metal as the flaps deployed and felt the vibration of hydraulics as the landing gear swung from the engine nacelles and locked with a bump. The plane swung to port. Youzek gathered the throttles in his right hand and pulled back as if he were reining in a team of panic-stricken horses. The cabin went platinum as the Lancaster settled into the searchlight beams, the WAAF's chant of "good luck, good luck, good luck" whispering in their headsets. M Mother scuffed the ground and, catching a crosswind, yawed to the right.

"Rudder, skipper," shouted Boog. "Try some rudder!"

The engines moaned with relief as Youzek settled her back into a three point landing. No one spoke as ground crew appeared, wearing silver haloes and throwing enormous silhouettes as they guided them to a pan where M Mother finally coughed herself still.

Silence hissed in his ears, sweet music after hours of battering by the engines. As the others began to tumble out the rear door, he made the operation's final entry in his log book.

"*Landed, South Wales, 0443 hrs. March 1, 1945.*"

Then he climbed down to the tarmac, where Rabbit and Darwinski lay on the concrete, kissing the ground. Thadeus wanted to do the same, but he wasn't sure he'd be able to get up again. Kadarek leaned jauntily against the tail fin. Seeing Thadeus, he held up his pack of Luckys and tossed him one.

Youzek dropped out of the forward hatch, drew his hands out of his gauntlets, and stood flexing his immense, life-saving fingers, then came back to stand at the head of their group. They stared into the glare of the searchlights and sucked in salt air leavened with petrol fumes. No one spoke until a jeep drew up abreast of them and a burly corporal jumped from behind the wheel and saluted.

"Is it heaven," Youzek asked, nodding into the fog as it resettled on the runway, "or the other place?"

"Neither, sir," replied the corporal in a cockney accent. "You're in St. David's. RAF St. David's. And may I be the first to wish you and your crew a happy St. David's Day."

IX

EVERYTHING TURNS TO VAPOUR as the overcast mixes with chimney smoke on the far side of the pond. Cremation. That's the ticket. He'll turn himself into smoke and blow east to Kingston, where John Kadarek worked as a TV repairman until he died of a heart attack at forty-five, then on toward the Atlantic. Maybe a few particles of himself will reach the Irish Sea to settle in England on the graves where Youzek, Prus, Bugajski, and Królik have also exhausted St. David's gift of years.

At Patterson's he'll tell the undertakers to divide the ashes: half to be buried with Marlene, half to go home. They'll fly him to Warsaw, where Darwinski, the fool, returned to die of his beatings in Pawiak prison, then his boys will take him back to Polesie.

"Come on," Thadeus mutters, "move yourself."

His legs feel ready to snap off at the knee as he extracts himself from Marlene's bench. He checks his watch. There's still time to trudge up to the funeral home. A cheap casket draped in one of Marlene's quilts, his medals on a cushion, two bouquets of roses, one red, one yellow, for his army regiment, a colour guard from the Air Force Association, white gloves and wedge caps and a foggy tape recording of the last post. Thadeus will make sure the undertakers have it all written down. Then he'll stop at Henry's Hardware. Buy garbage bags, start lightening his load for the long flight back.

Coming to Baranica

M orning sunlight tints the pine grove in the sepia hues that used to colour my hallucinations. Except for the obelisk. A grey slab in the black and white photographs I've been shown, it hangs in the trees, looking like a visitation in its coat of bright blue paint. My throat tightens when my cousin Ela says, "We are coming to Baranica."

I HAD DONE MY best to avoid getting here. It's fair to say Alex and I were both pretty messed up at Dad's funeral — hard not to be after the old boy stepped into Copernicus Avenue on a foggy March afternoon and walked straight into the path of an suv. Alex coped by playing man of the hour, looking after all the arrangements, parading down the aisle of St. Voytek's behind the coffin with his perfect family while I skulked behind and people in the packed pews whispered, "There he is, the pill-popper, the drunk, his mother's boy."

I coped by getting angry — at Dad. It was as if he'd walked into that Jeep with the express purpose of getting back at me for being the great disappointment in his life. Harsh, I know, completely selfish, but I was off my medication and back on the bottle. When I was through with Dad, I got angry at Alex, partly for being Alex, and mainly for playing the grand executor after the funeral, reading me Dad's last request like it was the Riot Act, then shoving a film canister holding some of his ashes into my hands, along with a one-way ticket to Warsaw and some traveller's cheques. He said I'd get the return ticket and the rest of my money when the deed was done.

I didn't let Alex drive me to the airport. I didn't want him to know I'd managed to swap my seat for one on a flight to Paris. I had decided to show Dad what I'd been up to all those years in Europe. I gave him a tour of Barbès-Rochechouart in Paris, enjoyed a few Sangria-soaked days in Madrid, smoked some skunk in the cafés of Amsterdam. At every stop, I sent Alex a postcard so that he knew exactly what I was up to. After Amsterdam, I wobbled around Germany for a few days, getting on trains at random, zigzagging eastwards until our cousin Ela scooped me up off the floor of the Wrocław train station. My bags had been stolen, but somehow I'd managed to hang on to my passport and the canister, which I'd kept in my jeans pocket.

Ela poured me into her little Fiat and swept me off to her place in Kleinsaltz. A nurse by trade, she had me clocked the minute she saw me. She took it all in stride, set me up in a bed of down comforters and crisp linen, and watched over my detox, using herbal remedies brewed by distant aunts until the meds a doctor friend had prescribed began to kick in.

After the shakes and the cold sweats had passed, she brought me album after album of faded photos. She showed me the pages as if they were ink blots in one of those tests they used to give me at the

Clarke in Toronto, and she taught me the names of the men and women posing stiffly in family portraits. I couldn't understand a word of what she said, but that didn't matter to Ela. She jabbered on regardless and, as my Copernicus Avenue Polish came back to me, I started taking on the things she was telling me about Polesie, Poland's vanished eastern marshes. She told me about the stillness of the place and how, on holy days, Dad's family would sing hymns into the marshes and the villagers in Karstwo, a settlement two miles away, would sing back to them. The peasants, who weren't Polish and weren't Russian either, called themselves *tutejsie*, "here people." They believed that our great grandfather, Gregory Mienkiewicz, had healing powers. He had founded Baranica with a lease from a Russian prince who was up to his ears in gambling debts. By the time Gregory died, the family were making sugar, clothing, and bread, from beets, flax, and grain grown on land that they had clawed back from the swamps. Ela told me how, the night he died in his sleep, our grandmother found Gregory hacking at the threshold of his bedroom with an axe. When she asked him what was wrong, Gregory tossed aside the axe, pointed at his room, and said, "I won't be needing it anymore."

Ela told me that my brother Alex is named after our grandfather, Aleksander Mienkiewicz, a sharp dresser and raconteur who had tried to emigrate before Dad was born. He was supposed to get work building railroads in the American West; instead, saloon keepers paid him to keep crowds of polacks in their bars with his jokes and stories, until his wife had to sell a cow to raise the fare to bring him back.

I had spent most of my life not knowing — and not wanting to know — about Baranica. When we were kids, we didn't even know the place had a name, or that it wasn't in Poland anymore. When Alex finally started asking him about it, the old man would just snarl at him and say, "There's nothing left in Baranica, and nothing to tell." It was one more thing he kept locked away from us, making us both feel like we were his consolation prize for not quite winning the war. Alex went back to him again and again with his questions, only to have the door slammed in his face. For me, the answer was to act as if I didn't give a shit.

It wasn't until I had Ela sitting on the edge of my bed, holding up her photos of the dead as if they had Gregory's magic powers, that I realized what an effort all that not-caring had been. It took three weeks for my Polish meds to take hold, then I was ready to do what had to be done.

We crossed into Belarus at Brest on the Bug River, negotiating our way through a three-kilometre queue of cars and trucks with the money Alex had sent to Ela. Then we cut south and east across fields of wheat, potatoes, and beets under a Saskatchewan-sized sky. As she drove, Ela explained how, before the war, this had been the biggest marshland in Europe, dotted with colonies like Baranica, whose farmers timed their crops to the rise and fall of water in the soil and whose oak forests, full of elk and wild boar, kept the family hidden while starving Tsarist, German, and Bolshevik armies pillaged their way back and forth across Polesie during Dad's boyhood. There's nothing left of that landscape now. The Soviets moved the border west and expelled most of the Poles who'd survived the Second World War, then drained the swamps and cut down the forest to make way for collective farms. On the highway east of Pinsk, Ela shouted and gesticulated every time we crossed a stream whorled with silver-green grasses or overhung with willows.

"There, Blez," she cried. "That is the real Polesie."

THIS IS IT. BARANICA. Mile one on the journey that was Dad's life. Gravel pops under the tires as the Fiat passes the blue monument among the pines that have replaced the old forest. Like everything else here, these new trees are just markers for something that no longer exists. The thatched houses of Dad's day have been replaced by Russian clapboard homes with shutters and gingerbread work. Ela points out each house as we pass, and names a vanished relative. "That's where your Uncle Władisław lived. This was Jakub Loziuk's farm. The Dąbrowskis were over there."

First stop is the site of our grandfather's homestead. It's just a wheat field now, but Ela points out the Linden tree that she says Dad climbed as a child at the side of the road. She says it's the one thing he always asked her mother about in his letters, so years ago Ela's mother made a pilgrimage here and hung a glass case containing an icon of Our Lady of Częstochowa in its branches. Ela has brought a new one, painted by her twelve-year-old grandson, and our first job is to replace it.

A sunburned woman in a headscarf and huge rubber boots shuffles out of the house across the road where, as Ela explains, the village school once stood. I can only make out a few words of the dialect that rolls like a stone in the woman's mouth. "People used to live in that field," she says. "Different people. A long time ago." We show her the icon and point to the tree and her son brings us a ladder made from rails of split cedar. Ela and I argue in broken phrases and the private sign language we've worked out between ourselves about whether I'm fit to climb the ladder. I win the argument. My hands are steady as they've felt in months as I lift the little case from its nail above the Linden's bottom-most limbs. The glass is fogged up with cobwebs and the husks of dead bugs. To help us clean it, the sunburned woman fetches a basin of tea-coloured water. "This is the best water in Baranica," she says. "You can drink this water!"

Ela takes the faded Madonna out of the case, cleans the glass, and slips in the new icon. I take the case back up, hang it on the nail. I take a minute to admire her grandson's handiwork: the fleur-de-lys pattern decorating the Madonna's robe, the shading and highlighting of her face, and the clean line of the incisions made by a Tartar sabre on her cheek all show amazing draftsmanship. It's obviously a family talent, the same one I've left squandered at the bottom of a thousand pints. Dad had it too. Back in Kleinsaltz, Ela showed me the hand-tooled and painted leather bindings he made for her photo albums — a talent he never admitted to when he was busy dismissing the sketches I drew of him as "scribblings."

Families pass in horse-drawn wagons as we work. Mothers and daughters in headscarves of cornflower blue, fathers and sons in peaked caps and shapeless jackets that look like they've come straight from the Crippled Civilians. The Fiat's trunk is full of used clothing for the villagers. We deliver them to an elderly couple who Ela knows from other visits. They invite us into their two-room house — a kitchen and a front room with beds and rolled mattresses where three generations of their family sleep. On winter nights, the very sick, the very young, or the very elderly can sleep in a crawl space on top of the large masonry oven. They offer us tea with honey and a bag of sunflower seeds in exchange for the clothes. Ela declines the tea and, after we leave, she warns me not to eat the seeds. We're not far from the "Zone of Exclusion," where no one has set foot and no crop has been safe to eat since the nuclear accident at Chernobyl.

We drive back out on the road we came in on, and park alongside a sign showing a hand-painted Madonna very different from the one we've hoisted into Dad's Linden. This is a socialist-realist Madonna, who shelters an infant as she glares at the viewer over a block of stubby Cyrillic text.

We get out our tools, candles, and flowers, take them into the pines, and cross a forest floor checkered with light and shade. The cemetery proper is in a clearing about fifty yards past the enclosure we're heading for. I feel a nip of the fear when its wrought iron crucifixes seem to wave at me, then I realize it's just the breeze toying with the white linen shawls draped over their cross-pieces. The enclosure is in deep shade, a raised rectangular bed, one hundred feet by twenty, surrounded by a knee-high picket fence. The blue, Soviet-era obelisk, crowned with a red star, stands at the far end of the bed, and the newer Polish monument of polished granite crouches about halfway down from it.

Four hundred and eighty people are buried here.

For centuries the swamps, the forests, and the soft sandy soil of Polesie here had been the settlers' best defence. Muscovites, Tartars, and the armies of Napoleon and the Kaiser had all gone around it rather than risk getting bogged down. But during World War Two, this was the worst place to be in all of Europe. The marshes were a partisan's playground and the Nazis were determined to make Polesie a test bed for their new death brigades trained in the art of mass execution.

I know the whole story now. Ela has told me how, on the night of November 9, 1942, a munitions train was blown up by partisans on a nearby line serving the eastern front. Villagers of a neighbouring Belarussian settlement told the SS that the Poles in Baranica were to blame. On the morning of November 13, a detachment of *Einsatzgruppen* — from the same force that had slaughtered twenty thousand Jews in Pinsk the year before — came out of the forest and surrounded the colony. They drove twenty-nine families from their homes and herded them into the school across from our grandfather's house. From there, men, women, and children were marched to this spot and machine-gunned into the mass grave that now lies inside the picket fence. My grandfather, who was seventy-five at the time, is here. So is my cousin Eugeniusz, who was two. So are my uncles Nikolai, Konstanty, and Władysław, along with their families.

This was all meadowland in 1942. Now the pines sigh and sway a hundred feet above me. "I like to think," says Ela, "that these trees are the people who died here."

I read the names carved into the granite: Dąbrowskis, Kuczynskis, Loziuks, Rajs, Zurawskis, and at least two dozen Mienkiewiczes. They took them out of the schoolhouse three at a time and marched them across the fields to where I'm standing. It went on for eleven hours. I try to imagine what it would have been like for them to sit on that schoolhouse floor, with heads between their knees and hands behind their backs, and wait for the shots after their husbands, wives, children, and grandchildren had been taken. I try to imagine the pleas and the prayers and the desperate bargains offered up to the soldiers on this very spot. I imagine all the things Dad must have imagined when his sister's letters finally caught up to him in England. This is what he was protecting us from with his silence, the same way mothers like that woman on the sign must have covered the eyes of their children as they were marched to the edge of the pit. He was shielding us from the knowledge that our own flesh and blood had been thought deserving of this, and from the twisted thought that Alex and I would never have been born if none of this had happened. Most of all, he was fighting off the feeling that his war had been for nothing and his real place had been here in this trench with his brothers, nieces, and nephews.

Standing under those pines, I finally understand why Dad said it was me who had to fulfill this last request. While Alex knocked patiently and persistently, it was me, with my rebellions and my phony indifference, who had kicked hardest against the door he'd kept shut. This last request of his hasn't been a punishment or a penance. It's his way of letting me in.

We lay our flowers and light our candles in front of the smaller stone that Ela and her mother erected after the fall of the Soviet

Union. I run my hand over the rough hewn edges that remind me of the Katyn monument back at the foot of Copernicus Avenue. I pick up the shovel and pry open the earth. Under a scalp of roots and rotted pine needles, the soil is a dazzling gold colour. It looks warm and welcoming, and it sparks a memory of walking with him in High Park when I was nine or ten. He scooped a handful of soil from a bank overhanging a creek and told me how it was like the earth in Polesie, the same yellow hue, dry and sandy, but rich to those who knew how to till and plant when the marshes were high.

I take the film canister from my pocket and pour out the fine, pale ash. Then I say goodbye to this part of him, the part that none of us were ever able to reach, the part of him that couldn't leave behind a place that history had tried so hard to erase. Then I let the earth close over him. I don't really pray. I just harmonize my thoughts with the wind as it hums its greeting high up in the pines.

Being Alex

I hadn't been on Copernicus Avenue since the morning of our father's funeral, when the limousine from G.W. Patterson's funeral home carried us down its length to St. Voytek's. Now it was spring, and the smell of the lake wafted up from Sunnyside to the corner of Howard Park. I lifted my nose and inhaled, half expecting to find the moist air sweetened with the scent of Rowntree's that had perfumed my walks to school with roasting cocoa. The chocolate factory, which had stood a few blocks over, by the railway tracks, was long gone. The castle-shaped Joy Oil station had been replaced years ago by a Seven-11. The stuffy facade of the old TD Bank now framed a home furnishing studio that sold white furniture. The Revue Cinema was still going, though stripped of its marquee, and next to it sat the Café Bambi, long abandoned by Old Poniatowski and his circle of exiles, its string of faded flags gathering dust in the front window.

The Bambi was in darkness, except for the blue flicker of a television set, which suggested that Susie, the Thai woman who had taken over the place in the seventies, still presided there, the back half of the café serving as a living area from which she could keep watch on her rare customers while doing her ironing. If there was anything happening that night at the Bambi, I was too early. I had lost all sense of the late hours that people like Janiz kept.

The only explanation for the effect Janiz's phone calls had had was that they caught me at a vulnerable time. It was shock that had gotten me through our father's death and its aftermath. I had done my duty, just as I'd always done. I dealt with the doctors and the lawyers, made sure that Patterson's carried out the funeral arrangements exactly as he stipulated. Then I executed his will, distributed his bequests, and, feeling more than a little smug, read Blaise the terms of his inheritance. Blaise, I was pretty sure, had only come home to make sure he got what was coming to him, so he could go back to Europe and squander it — the same way he'd done with the money our Auntie M-K had left him four years before.

I took some grim satisfaction in watching the effect the will had on Blaise, but I was bewildered too. I was the dependable one, a full partner in my firm, a specialist in leveraged buyouts. I'd done everything I could to meet his expectations — got my MBA and my CA, married a good Polish girl, bought a big house overlooking Grenadier Pond. To me, our father's choice of Blaise to take his ashes back to Baranica was a reminder that none of it had been good enough.

Blaise behaved true to form, changing his ticket behind my back, taunting me with his postcards from Paris and Madrid. That's when Janiz's calls began.

"Alex Mienkiewicz?"

"Speaking."

"Can you explain what makes you such a self-centred prick? Fuck you."

It was a case of mistaken identity. She'd mislaid the number of the Alex Mienkiewicz she was looking for and I was the only one in the book. Any other time, I would have accepted her apology and hung up, but I was intrigued by the idea of there being another Alex Mienkiewicz out there, and Janiz was eager to tell me all about him. A performance artist, musician, poet, a world traveller — he was all the things Blaise and I had once thought we would be.

"I'm the unofficial president of his unofficial fan club," she said. "It's my unofficial way into his pants."

She told me this other Alex appeared regularly at the cafés and bistros that had opened up along Copernicus Avenue, and offered to keep me informed. I found myself waiting for Janiz to call while Therese put the kids to bed before adjourning to her study to review her case notes. She'd ring every couple of weeks with an invitation to one of Alex's performances and I'd ply her for information about his life on Copernicus Avenue, which had uncannily paralleled my own.

"Funny you never met," said Janiz when I pointed out how parallel our childhoods had run.

"Maybe it's just as well we haven't. What is it that they say happens when you meet your double?"

"One of you vanishes," she said.

I never did attend one of Alex Mienkiewicz's performances, but I invited Janiz to dinner, just once, a discreet rendezvous at Giorgio's on Bloor Street, away from the neighbourhood, where no one would recognize me.

"So?" she said after extending a hand as firm as any that I'd shaken. "Now you have to tell me how I'm nothing like what you expected."

She was exactly what I had expected, with a skirt printed with suns and moons and a belt buckle in the shape of a salamander. She wore her dyed black hair spiked up in a clip that looked like an instrument of torture. "What about me?" I asked. "I hope I'm not too much of a disappointment."

"Alex," she said, "I'm never disappointed."

Janiz lashed the room with a gaze that scorched everything it touched — the white tablecloths, overturned wine glasses, water goblets stuffed with fan-folded linen. As she worked her way through the most expensive items on the menu, I regaled her with my adventures in private equity, wishing I could find a way to communicate to her that I was capable of everything that she implied in her fetching glances.

"So let me get this straight," she said through a mouthful of tartufo at the end of my speech. "You guys are kind of like corporate buzzards. You let companies go bankrupt, then buy them so you can fire everyone and hire them back to do more work for less pay. Sounds skanky to me."

An explanation of our vital economic role as preservers of the residual wealth in dysfunctional enterprises would have been lost on her, so I carded the meal, walked her to High Park subway station, and bid her farewell with a chaste handshake.

There were no more phone calls after that and I missed them. I could never have been unfaithful to Therese, but the prospect of a transgression, of letting some part of my life spin out of control, had cut through the numbness that followed our father's death. So I kept pricking myself with the thought of there being another Alex Mienkiewicz out there, doing what I could have done while I spent my life compensating for my father's losses. That's what finally brought me back to Copernicus Avenue.

I stood with my nose pressed to the darkened window of the

Café Bambi, trying to discern my name on the makeshift posters that wrinkled behind the dirty glass. It wasn't there, so I crossed the street and let gravity pull me down toward the lake.

I'm not a nostalgic person. The Copernicus Avenue we had grown up on had been a dowdy, earnest, working neighbourhood for dowdy, earnest, working people. Lately, it has become the street that Blaise and I had wanted it to be when we were young. The trees planted twenty years ago send sprays of bud into the streetcar wires. Yola Skarpinski's bookstore, where we drank green teas, smoked Sobranies in wooden cigarette holders, and held clumsy discussions about the works of Colette, closed for lack of customers before we finished university, but now there are four bookstores — new, used, and antiquarian — thriving in the blocks above St. Bridget's Church. There is a store that sells antibiotic-free meats and one that dispenses holistic medicines. There's a cheese boutique, a daycare for dogs, shops that offer furniture made of teak and brushed steel, and others that display Buddhist tapestries and bright woollens from Ecuador and Nepal.

As I walked, soft jazz spilled from the roll-up doors of wine bars and, while the ghost of Monsignor Doyle still glowered at me from the stone porch of St. Bridget's Church, its columns were hung with coloured banners representing the Four Directions of its new First Nations congregation.

I tried to fix the name and image of each sharp new shop in my mind, but the old landmarks refused to relinquish their places: the Four Aces Grill, once presided over by a Cantonese patriarch in pigtail and silk coat, his wife hobbling between tables with plates of grilled cheese and chop suey; Isidore's Variety, later known as Boss's, later known as Pete's, where Blaise treated me to my first, only, and unsuccessful adventure in shoplifting; Walt's haberdashery, whose top hats, fedoras, and black bowlers, hovered on wire stands and convinced four-year-old me that the shop window was inhabited by invisible men.

Little details unlocked the Avenue in my head, like the brass spigot that still protrudes from the front corner of the Loblaws store — later an A&P, then a Red & White, now an IGA — where we used to tie up our dog alongside the hobo we called Inkman, who sat on the pavement selling pencils and pretending to have been crippled in the war. Overhead, the storefronts' upper storeys wore the same chipped fenestrations, amphoras, floral bosses, and curlicued entablature that I had tried to decode as a boy.

The side streets — Grenadier, Westminster, Fermanagh, Hanford, Wright, Garland — opened out with their newly renovated houses ranged like cakes in the window of Madame Wysotska's bakery. I looked down their colonnades of chestnut and maple and imagined coalmen covered in soot and icemen lugging crystal blocks in callipers to the doors of the very elderly. I saw the shade of the man we called Merlin on account of his flowing white beard, sidelocks, and robe, the last of the city's rag and bone men on his wagon drawn by a blinkered nag.

I passed under Lech's bay window, hanging over the pavement like a shuttered icon opposite the cement rosettes of St. Voytek's. I'd heard he was back in Poland, this "nowhere" place in the New World having proved as much of a disappointment to him as had my discipleship. At the corner of Hanford and Copernicus, I found Babayaga's phone booth replaced by a Plexiglas sleeve that wouldn't shelter a mouse. The bag lady had died years ago in the fire that consumed the old Sunnyside Station building on a flat car in the yards south of Queen Street. With any luck, she found renewed peace in heaven with the arrival of His Holiness John Paul II, the feet of whose statue outside the Parish Trust were still littered with flowers, though it had been weeks since his passing in Rome.

In the block south of Garland, I stopped in my tracks and stared into the window of Sobieski's menswear. This was the only storefront unchanged from the time of my daily walks home from St. Bridget's School — the weathered lettering of its hand-painted sign barely discernible. The window was all but empty, save for a headless mannequin that sported a sack-like pair of brown, pinstripe trousers, a beige shirt with wide tie striped in earth tones, and a shapeless drab windbreaker: the uniform of a generation of men who have all but disappeared from the Avenue. A semicircle of women's cashmere berets, the kind my mother had always favoured, lay unwanted at the mannequin's feet.

From there, it was a short drift to the bottom of Copernicus Avenue. I passed the Edgewater Hotel, where Blaise had begun his disintegration and whose patrons, believing I was an undercover cop, had given me the cold shoulder when I came looking for him. My brother Blaise: always late, frequently absent, prone to disappear when you wanted him most. Blaise, who had scattered his talents to the four winds, who refused to make something of himself as if it were some kind of moral principle. As I came to the bottom of the Avenue, where Queen and King streets tie themselves off in a knot of wire and rails, I realized how much my father's son I'd been, how much I had needed to believe that Blaise could have shaken off the darkness that had consumed our mother if he'd just followed Dad's exhortations to "move yourself."

I crossed King Street to where the Katyn monument is planted at the Avenue's root. A monolith of cast bronze, riven in two as if by lightning, it commemorates the four thousand Polish officers murdered by the Soviets in the Katyn Forest in the spring of 1940, each one taken to the edge of a mass grave, hands bound in barbed wire, a ligature round the neck, and shot through the back of the head. Blaise had refused to attend the monument's dedication. I thought it was childish of him, a spiteful way to get back at the old man. Now I understood it; he just couldn't accept that our whole life had to be defined by the fissure in that bronze block and the disconnection it represented.

On the way back up the other side of Copernicus Avenue, I stopped only once, at the corner opposite St. Voytek's where Dad had stepped off the curb on the first day of March. Without his hearing aid, he didn't hear the oncoming car when he took a step back from the centre line to let a streetcar pass. Therese had told me that, every other week, someone had been taping two bundles of roses, one yellow, one red, to the hydro pole at that corner. The last of these bouquets was wilting on the post as I drew up to it.

I took them down and put them in the bin. It was over. I had the last of Blaise's postcards in my breast pocket. It had been sent from Pinsk, with a stamp bearing the image of St. Euphrosyne of Polatsk. Dad's will had been done. My brother was coming home.

Acknowledgements

THANKS TO MARC CÔTÉ for his faith in this book and the sound judgment that has made it a better one, to Angel Guerra for a fine cover, and to everyone at Cormorant for their hard work.

Grain magazine got the ball rolling by publishing "Twelve Versions of Lech," which led to its subsequent publication in *The Journey Prize Stories 19*. Kim Jernigan and the team at *The New Quarterly* not only published "An Offering" and "Babayaga," but also provided constructive feedback and encouragement that has sustained me for many years.

Thanks to Laura Jones for the pics, to the Grayceful Daddies for the soundtrack, and to Zero Horse Town for the help and shared madness. Franklin Carter, Susan Girvan, Don Loney, Kathleen Dowling, Jerry McGrath, and Jerry Silverberg all vetted early versions of these stories. Leon Evans at the Canadian Warplane Heritage Museum counselled me on the ups and downs of piloting a Lancaster bomber. This book would not have been possible without the support of the Ontario Arts Council, the Toronto Arts Council, and the Canada Council for the Arts.